Readers love
ANDREW GREY

All for You

"*All for You* is now hands-down my favorite Andrew Grey book… so far."

—Gay Book Reviews

"…Andrew Grey always comes up with something new and enlightening."

—Paranormal Romance Guild

Don't Let Go

"I highly recommend this book. It's sexy, sweet, and Robert and Zeke will capture your heart. I'd have loved to be able to spend more time with them, and I think you'll feel the same."

—Joyfully Jay

"I gladly recommend this book. It was a beautiful ballad, the kind you hummed with a secret smile on your lips."

—OptimuMM

Fire and Granite

"*Fire and Granite* is another suspenseful and tension filled installment in the Carlisle Deputies series. The plot has plenty of danger and suspicious characters along with two sweet kids and a cute dog."

—The Novel Approach

"Adventure, excitement, fascination, hot sexy times, danger and so much more is what you will find in this book. It caught my attention from the start and kept it all the way to the end."

—MM Good Book Reviews

More praise for
ANDREW GREY

Running to You

"As always Andrew has outdone himself with this story. I urge you to go out and get your copy so you can get lost in Carlos and Billy Joe's world."

—Love Bytes

"Andrew Grey always manages to pull at my heartstrings in so many ways. This book is no exception…"

—Diverse Reader

Smoldering Flame

"Andrew Grey did such an amazing job on this book. It is truly an emotional read."

—Gay Book Reviews

"This is a beautiful story…"

—Paranormal Romance Guild

Buried Passions

"The story blends in interesting themes of prejudice, and not just homophobia. The anti-immigrant sentiment was dealt with in a realistic way. And the Big City versus small town mentality was handled well, too."

—Joyfully Jay

"…this is a well written low angst love story."

—Open Skye Book Reviews

By ANDREW GREY

Pulished by DREAMSPINNER PRESS
www.dreamspinnerpress.com

Pulished by DREAMSPINNER PRESS
www.dreamspinnerpress.com

UNFAMILIAR WATERS

ANDREW GREY

Published by
DREAMSPINNER PRESS

5032 Capital Circle SW, Suite 2, PMB# 279, Tallahassee, FL 32305-7886 USA
www.dreamspinnerpress.com

Unfamiliar Waters
© 2019 Andrew Grey.

Cover Art
© 2019 Kanaxa.
Cover content is for illustrative purposes only and any person depicted on the cover is a model.

Trade Paperback ISBN: 978-1-64080-965-9
Digital ISBN: 978-1-64080-964-2
Library of Congress Control Number: 2018956966
Trade Paperback published January 2019
v. 1.0

Printed in the United States of America
∞
This paper meets the requirements of
ANSI/NISO Z39.48-1992 (Permanence of Paper).

To Tricia and Lynn—
their encouragement and hours on the phone
really helped this story pay off!

CHAPTER 1

A SHOT split the air, and Garrett Wreckley crouched behind the fence post directly in line with the front door of the dilapidated wood-sided home. Once, it might have housed a family who raised their kids, went to work, and did their best to get by. But that was a different decade... a different time. Now death and decay infested the place, drugs rotting the people on the inside and spreading their disease outward as far as the inhabitants could push it.

"Come out and you won't be hurt," one of the negotiators called from behind him. Garrett didn't have the time to worry about who it was. His head went in a million directions at a time like this. Garrett needed to stop this mind-wandering shit and focus.

The answer was another shot, this one away from him. Other officers swarmed around the sides of the building, giving the inhabitants a wide berth until it was time to move in. Garrett waited for the go-ahead and then the smash of doors as officers swarmed the house. With a wild yell, he raced up the walk and crashed through the front door like the Hulk. The front room was empty, so he went to the next.

A man, stoned out of his mind, sat in the corner of the dining room, trying to get his legs under him.

"Stay down!" When the man continued his efforts to stand, Garrett pointed his gun at him. "I said, stay down." Blood flooded with endorphins and testosterone, fueled by enough caffeine to wire an elephant, raced through his veins. His finger already on the trigger, he repeated his call, ready to shoot. Garrett's hand shook just a little as his gaze narrowed to a pinpoint. He'd blow him away in a split second if the idiot didn't listen. "Just give me a reason," Garrett whispered under his breath.

"The house is secure…," a voice came through his radio, but Garrett ignored it. The man in front of him—small, painfully thin—rose but stayed in the corner. Garrett didn't lower his gun at all.

"Hey, I have him," Coleridge half whispered.

Garrett didn't move, not looking away from the dirty, scraggly man for a second.

A hand touched his shoulder, pulling Garrett out of the spell he'd been under. His vision returned to normal, and Garrett began breathing once again.

"It's all right. I have him. The guy is completely stoned."

Garrett slowly lowered his weapon. Without a word, he let Coleridge take the man into custody, holstered his gun, and left the house. He didn't speak to anyone as he walked through the sea of police cruisers until he got to his own, where he sat behind the wheel, heart still racing but slowly returning to normal. He started the engine and turned the air-conditioning to full blast to try to cool his skin and evaporate the sweat that was everywhere.

After a few minutes, Garrett put the car in gear and headed through the streets of Baltimore and back into the station.

"Good bust," one of the guys said as Garrett passed. He answered blankly, going right to the computer at his desk to write up his report. Not that he had a great deal to say, but he got it done and sent off before finally allowing himself to take a deep breath and a look around.

The station was about as old as Garrett felt—damned near ancient, even though he was only twenty-nine. Not that it fucking mattered in the least.

His phone rang and he snatched it up.

"Get in here," the captain growled, and for a second, Garrett wondered what had crawled up his ass. Then he realized it was probably him and swore under his breath. "Now!"

"On my way," Garrett answered blankly, and headed to the captain's office in the nicer portion of the building. He rapped lightly on the door and entered at the call.

"Shut the door," Captain Rodriguez said, and Garrett complied, taking a seat across from him. "You are out of control." The captain was in his midforties, with intelligence radiating from his eyes like a beacon—one Garrett didn't particularly want shining on him at the moment.

"Excuse me…?" Garrett asked.

"You nearly shot an unarmed suspect crouching in a damned corner. The guy was harmless, and yet every officer on the damned task force heard you yelling at him. The guy already had his damned hands in the air and had peed himself, and you stood there with him at gunpoint like you were fucking Rambo. Wreckley, you're a complete mess and out of fucking control. I checked your duty roster, and you haven't worked less than sixty hours a week in six months. To say you're burned out is an understatement. You're a damned husk and running on coffee and goddamned Cheetos. You have to get your shit together, and you need to do it now."

"I will, sir." Maybe some real food and a good night's sleep would help. Hell, maybe he could find a little company and spend some time at a club. A day off actually sounded pretty good.

"You're damned right. You have several weeks of vacation, and you're going to use some of it. I expect you to fill out a request in the next half hour, and I don't want to see your ass in here for at least a month."

Garrett swallowed. "A month?" What the hell was he going to do for an entire month? He barely kept ahead of the ghosts chasing him as it was, and now… a fucking month on vacation, with hours to think? He would go fucking crazy.

"Yes."

"What do I do?" Garrett asked a little absently, not intending to say anything out loud.

"I don't know." The captain's voice softened a little, but not much. "You grew up here, and as I remember, you said once you used to sail. Rent a damned boat and sail around for a while, who knows? Do I look like a travel agent? Go somewhere warm, to a resort, sit on the beach, watch men parade around in rainbow thongs or whatever it is you like. I don't know. But as of right now, you're on vacation and barred from the building for a month, so go set something up, figure some shit out, and when you come back, have your head screwed on right or I'll have to find a shrink who'll do it for you, and you don't want that on your record." He picked up a file, and Garrett took that for a dismissal.

He left the office and went back to his desk, complying with the captain's directive and requesting vacation time, grumbling under his breath the entire time.

"Heard the bust went really well," Brent Ogilvie said as he perched on the edge of Garrett's desk, flashing Garrett a bright come-hither smile. Brent hadn't been shy about his attraction, and he was adorable… at least he would be under most circumstances to many people. He had huge, wide, puppy-dog eyes in deep brown, a mouth perfect for work down south, and a head of hair as black as night that was always going in a million directions, but on him it was perfection. Not that Garrett had really noticed—much—or cared.

"I think it did. Others have their opinion." Garrett yanked open his desk drawer and nearly dumped the entire thing on the floor. He stared into it and then closed it harder than he needed to.

"You know…." Brent shifted to give Garrett a better look at the goods. "I'm off in an hour…." He cocked his eyebrow slightly and arched his back just a bit, leaving little to interpretation.

"I'm heading out now, and I'm on vacation for the next month." Garrett paused, thinking that Brent might not be a bad way to start.

Maybe a little time getting off would be good. But as messed up and stressed as he was, even he knew that getting involved with Brent Ogilvie in any way was a huge mistake. The guy had long-term relationship written all over him, and Garrett was already married… in his heart.

"I appreciate the kind words, but I have to get out of here before the captain chops my nuts off. I'll see you in a month." He grabbed his old canvas backpack, slung it over his shoulder, turned off his computer, and hurried out of the station before anyone else stopped him. The rumor mill would fill them in quickly enough, and since he was on vacation, he wasn't going to have to be around to hear what it came up with.

HIS HOME, what remained of it, resided in the Mount Vernon section of town. It had been David's dream. Now it was hollow. Garrett's footsteps echoed on the parquet floors and through rooms devoid of life. At one time Garrett had dreams too, but now he just existed, without a damn thing he could do about it. He'd been left to pick up the pieces, and all things considered, Garrett thought he was doing pretty well. Of course, that was his opinion and everyone else could go to hell, so it wasn't necessarily unbiased.

The downstairs rooms were largely closed. They were furnished, and someone from a service came in and dusted, but he never used them. Garrett kept the french doors to those rooms shut and never even turned his head as he walked through the entrance hall to the stairs.

In his bedroom, he closed the door and turned on the television. Clothes adorned just about every available space, so Garrett grabbed a basket from the floor of the closet, scooped everything into it, and took the back stairs down to the kitchen and laundry area. He shoved the clothes into the machine and got it going. Some fucking vacation: doing the laundry he'd neglected for weeks and searching through the refrigerator for something edible and finding nothing. He slammed the door shut, opened the nearest drawer in the granite-topped island, and grabbed a take-out menu that looked interesting. He made a call, and soon food was on the way.

Garrett pulled out one of the stools from under the counter, perched himself on it, and opened the laptop he kept there. He hated this room. It was beautiful and gleaming, with white counters, a professional stove, and a stainless double refrigerator. It was gorgeous... and he couldn't stand it, hated sitting in it. The kitchen had been David's domain, and now it sat empty. Well, not exactly empty. The drawers and cabinets were full, perfectly organized, and exactly as David had left them.

He googled vacation getaways, and pictures with people boating, happy and having a good time, filled his screen. God, the thought of all those people, yammering and yapping on and on about nothing, made his stomach clench. Though the boating thing might not be so bad. David could get seasick in the bathtub, so Garrett hadn't been on the water in years, though he did know how to sail. He pulled up a map and started looking around for an out-of-the-way place that was warm. Then he searched for boat rentals and made a few calls. By the time his dinner arrived, he had a plan, and before he could finish his kung pao chicken, he had a reservation and plane ticket. Damn, God bless the internet. All he had to do was get to the airport on time.

Life, especially his, was never quite that simple. He had to call the cleaning company to let them know he'd be away, though he didn't cancel the appointment since they had a key, and his neighbors so they could make sure the house looked lived in and get his mail.

Just one last call to make.

"Jilly, I'm going on vacation," he told his sister when she answered.

"Jesus Christ, it's about fucking time," she blurted, then groaned as he heard his niece in the background.

"What's fucking time, Mommy?" At four, Nikki repeated everything.

"Nothing, honey. Why don't you go watch *Dora*? I'll be in there in a minute," Jilly said, sounding on the edge as well. "Mike has been on a business trip for a week, and I'm about ready to climb the walls. Is there any way I can go on this vacation with you?" Her tone said she was kidding, but not. Mike was not one of Garrett's favorite people, and he'd gone so far as to run a background check on the guy to see if there was anything he could use to get him lost and never to be found. No such luck. It wasn't that Mike was such a bad guy, but Jilly spent a lot of time home alone while he was gallivanting around the world, and his family needed him.

"Sure. Grab the kids, leave your husband, and come spend the next month with me on a sailboat." He was joking, but Jilly sighed wistfully, as though tempted. "Anyway, would you stop by the house and make sure nothing happens to it and shit?"

She paused. "You're really doing the sailboat thing? We haven't done that since we were in college. Good for you. Do Mom and Dad know?"

He groaned. "Really? Like I'm going to announce to them that I'm going. I can just hear Mom. 'Oh, that beautiful house of yours is going to be empty. I think your father and I will come into the city for a few days.'" He pitched his voice higher, doing a pretty good impression of his mom. "By the time I got home, the place would be a disaster, with every dish piled in the sink, everything a complete mess, and them nowhere to be found because they left two days earlier." He knew exactly what would happen because it had before. "And if Mom and Dad do find out, I changed the alarm passcode." He gave it to her. "If you pass it on, I will have to kill you."

"Got it." Jilly knew firsthand how their mother was. Being the youngest, she had gotten the full brunt of their mom's laziness and the guilt she could lay on anyone who tried to point that fact out to her. "You will call me while you're gone?"

"I'll try. It isn't like there's cell service on the water, but I plan to island-hop for a while, and I'll call you when I dock. And of course, you can tell Nikki and Davey...." Every time he thought of his one-year-old nephew, he choked. Jilly had named him after David, and.... He didn't need to go there. "I'll find some cute things for the kids." Garrett really liked being the favorite uncle. Actually, he was the only uncle, but details... details.

"When are you leaving?"

"Tomorrow morning. There was a seat on a flight out of BWI to St. Thomas. From there I'm heading south, and I'll pick up the boat in Barbados." Sun, warmth, sand, quiet—they all called to him. He needed them like he needed air and water.

"You can count on me to keep my mouth shut. Just have a good time, and don't forget us landlubbers up north, freezing our bits off." She laughed as Nikki fussed in the background about being hungry. "And I won't say anything to Mom and Dad. But you should call them. They miss you."

"I will, but not until I can talk to them without grinding my teeth and wanting to argue with every boneheaded thing Mom says simply because she either thinks it's funny or cute." There was no way he could take that right now. His mother didn't have opinions. She changed her mind depending on whoever she and his dad were with, and she could say the stupidest things just because it was what she thought someone she wanted to like her wanted to hear.

Nikki was having some kind of breakdown or tantrum in the background, so Garrett figured it was time to go.

"I'll talk to you soon. You take care of yourself. And kick Mike in the nuts if he isn't helping you." Jilly let him get away with doing too little as far as Garrett was concerned.

Jilly laughed. "I may just do that. But he's promised me he'll be home for the next couple of months, so I'll have some help, and no matter what you think of him, Mike is a great dad."

When he is home. Garrett didn't say that part, just told her goodbye and hung up the phone.

It was already late and he still had to pack and arrange for a ride to the airport. With a sigh, he slid off the stool, shut down the small laptop, and slid it into his backpack. Then he returned upstairs, found some luggage—purposely ignoring that it had been David's—and set to work.

CHAPTER 2

AFTER TWO days of flights, ironing out agreements, a demonstration of the features of the forty-foot sailboat, and loading supplies and water, Garrett was on his way. The air was clean, the breeze crisp and gentle, the sky a blue that could only represent serenity and calm. A scant eight hours away from Barbados, Garrett was heading north and everything was perfection. He stayed on the leeward side of the islands in the Caribbean, rather than the Atlantic, and plotted a course to nowhere in particular.

Eight hours and he could already feel some of the tension slipping away. Garrett inhaled deeply and followed the track laid out by the satellite navigation system. His radar showed nothing but bright skies and clear sailing as far as he could see, and there were no reports of any bad weather, other than a light shower, within hundreds of miles. Garrett couldn't ask for more.

He sat on the cabin housing with the sunshade up, his hands on the wheel, watching the horizon. Barbados had disappeared into the distance, and he set a course northwest toward St. Lucia. He hadn't decided if he would even stop there, but being close to an island in case he needed help was probably a good idea. The ocean could be a dangerous, unforgiving place.

Garrett reached for his hat and plopped it onto his head, his eyes hidden behind sunglasses. With so much glare off the crystal clear water, he could damage his eyes, and he didn't want that. All he wanted was peace, and he was getting that in spades.

Garrett went to his cooler, dug out a soda, and popped it open before grabbing a sandwich. He'd figured the sail to St. Lucia was about ten to eleven hours, and he had three or so more to go. Then he could figure out where he'd head from there.

"This is the life," he said to no one. A gull zoomed overhead, following him, a sure sign he was approaching land. It dipped and soared over the water and probably contemplated how to swoop in to steal Garrett's sandwich. "This is mine, you flying rat," he teased as the gull kept up with him. It was comforting, like having a silent companion, someone else with him who didn't require his constant attention or for him to talk.

Land grew on the horizon as he skimmed over the water, the wind picking up, carrying him faster than he expected. Not that he was complaining. Garrett navigated to the leeward side of the island and found a secure, deserted-looking cove to anchor the boat, then went belowdecks. Out of the sun, he sat on one of the benches to decide what to have for dinner.

Garrett ended up having a fried pork chop, along with cold fruit and veggies. It was perfect, and when followed by a beer or two and a nap in the shade as the sun slid beneath the horizon, his weary mind could almost forget what he'd had and lost.

He found he had cell service from his position, so he made a call to Jilly. "Hey, sister," he said when she answered. "Greetings from St Lucia."

"You didn't sink," she teased. "How is the boat?"

"Nice. I was expecting a tub, but it's not very old, sleek, and beautifully appointed. I snagged it after a last-minute cancellation. The bed is really nice." He nearly said David would have liked it… well, once he'd gotten over his seasickness. Still, David had never been one to let anything stop him, and if Garrett had suggested a trip like this, he probably would have gone to make Garrett happy.

"I know…," she said softly.

"What do you know?" he asked too harshly and way too quickly.

"That you still miss him. Hell, I know that you haven't slept in the room the two of you shared since he passed away. You try to act all tough, but I know that losing David ripped you apart. But, big brother, it's time you pulled yourself together and stopped this aloof, strong-man asshole demeanor and figured out how you are going to live the rest of your life."

Garrett sighed. "You don't take it easy on a guy, do you?" Not that he would have expected her to. Even when they were kids, Jilly had dished it out as well as she took it. Jilly got even... and when she did, you knew it. That girl had the patience to watch a turtle marathon.

Jilly laughed like a supervillain. "Never have, never will. It's my job—just like it's yours to point out when I'm being a pushover. And now that I've given you a kick in the butt, I'm going to hang up and try to make up for being grouchy to my husband."

"You go on. I'm going to go scrub out my brain rather than think about what that entails." He laughed as he ended the call. There was still enough light to see, so Garrett changed into a bathing suit, lowered the rope off the back of the boat, and slid into the water to cool off.

Garrett loved how salt water felt like liquid velvet on his skin. He didn't swim, exactly, because darkness fell quickly, and when it did, there would be nothing for him to see by. Instead, he hung on the edge of the boat, just letting the water flow around him luxuriously. More and more stars came out, and eventually he climbed up to lie on the deck in the warm evening air, looking at the billions of stars that split the night and the meteors that shot across the sky.

"If you can hear me, David, I miss you," he said into the darkness before picking out a single point of light. When he was a kid, his grandmother had told him that all the people we love turned into stars when they passed on. He knew that wasn't true, of course, but it was a lovely thought, so he picked out a star for David. "I don't know why you had to leave me, but I've been total shit since you did. I don't like anything or anyone." He sighed and lay still, wondering if he could somehow hear David's voice on the wind.

Now he was descending into some kind of bad Nicholas Sparks romantic drivel. "I know you're gone and this is just me talking to myself, but that doesn't mean I don't miss you and that I don't want you back." He closed his eyes as a wave of grief reared up. For months he'd held firm, building huge, thick walls to try to keep it out, but this time his defenses were down, and it broke over him like a tidal wave. Garrett rolled onto his side and heaved, yelling his grief and pain out into the blackness and over the water. "You were too fucking young, and we should have had decades together." He grabbed for the towel and plastered it to his eyes to catch his tears and keep them from showing. Even enveloped in darkness, he didn't want to be seen like this.

Garrett lost track of how long he lay like that, eventually dozing off. He woke to discomfort and went below, turning on the lights to find his way. Garrett hung up his wet things in the tiny bathroom and went to bed. He fell asleep on top of the covers and didn't wake until a beam of sunlight shone on his face. He'd slept—at least that was an improvement, and it hadn't required six beers or three or four shots to lull him into dreamland.

He lay in bed, the boat rocking, water lapping the side. Then he got up and ate a cold breakfast before deciding to move on. He had plenty of provisions, so he didn't need to dock, and the open water called to him. After eating, he checked the weather and set a course for Martinique. He'd already made arrangements for a berth there for a few days, so off he went, back out into the huge blue expanse, his heart a little lighter and his outlook maybe a little brighter. After all, it was always more beautiful after a storm, and maybe that included the emotional kind as well.

AFTER NOON, clouds built to the east and the wind picked up. Garrett checked his timing and bearings, set the wheel, and added additional sail to pick up speed. The radar showed some sort of storm heading his way, though it could be possible for him to outrun it.

The two islands were only twenty-five miles apart, so no more than three hours out of St. Lucia, he should be spying land at any time. Garrett scanned the horizon and his GPS as he sped over the water. The waves picked up with the wind as the storm drew closer. Most Caribbean storms were small and mainly dumped rain, but this one must have some oomph. It didn't appear to be big, but it was packing some wind.

With still about an hour to go by his calculations, he spied land off to the west. Rather than questioning it, he headed that way.

The island was small, definitely not Martinique. The chart listed it as Montessa. Not that he'd ever heard of it. Didn't matter, though. The clouds drew closer and closer to the water as he approached the north side of the island. He found a break in the reef and slipped into a small cove. The water instantly calmed, and he breathed a sigh of relief. After dropping anchor, he lowered the sails and stowed them away, then closed all the windows, as well as the access hatch. He wasn't sure exactly what he was in for, but when the rain hit, it was torrential. The boat rocked side to side, but not badly, and he stood under shelter, setting out some clean buckets to catch the fresh water.

After the thunder and lightning passed, Garrett stripped down, grabbed a bar of soap, and washed himself off, letting the rain rinse him clean.

Once done, Garrett went inside, dried off, dressed, and made himself dinner, listening to the rain pound the roof of the cabin overhead. The batteries were charged and he'd used very little the night before, so he settled on the bed to read, passing the hours quietly until it was time to sleep.

Sometime in the night, the storm passed, leaving behind quiet, and again Garrett slept soundly. He hadn't dreamed, at least not that he remembered.

In the morning, other than being wet, the boat was fine. He ate a cold breakfast and then ventured onto the deck. He stood, scanning over the island for any signs of habitation. He saw nothing but thick vegetation and a small lagoon nearer to shore. He thought he might explore it and moved the boat closer inland. With no one around and a sandy beach, he figured it was safe for a swim ashore to have a look around.

Garrett dressed for the water and sun in his suit and a solar shirt before venturing back out. He'd planned to jump off the side of the boat for the swim to shore, but when movement near the beach caught his eye, he paused on deck.

A man stepped out of the trees, blond and tall, sun-kissed, wearing a pair of shorts and a gray T-shirt that he pulled over his head as he got closer to the water. Garrett watched the gorgeous creature move with unusual grace before stopping, and knew the minute the man spotted the boat—he stopped to look and then waved. Garrett waved back, still just watching and wishing he had his binoculars. The man waded into the water as though looking for something, then dove, swimming strongly when he came up before diving again, surfacing with a large conch shell. He paddled to shore, looked it over, then dove back into the water and came up without it.

This time when he broke the surface, the man waved again and motioned him over. Garrett contemplated only a minute before diving into the water, heading straight to shore. After all, some god of the water didn't beckon him every day of the week. Even as he swam, Garrett wondered if he'd imagined the whole thing. It wasn't until he stepped out of the water and the man approached that he was sure he was real.

"Hi," he said brightly. "I'm Nigel, Nigel Martin."

"Garrett Wreckley. I got caught in the storm last night and found the cove for shelter." He looked around again. "Do you think the owner will mind if I stay here?"

Nigel smiled and shrugged. "It's okay. He isn't going to mind, since it's me… well, sort of. But it's fine. No one is going to know you're here. As long as you don't tear up the reef or harm my friends under the water, it will be okay." He flashed perfect teeth, a gorgeous smile, and had eyes bluer and with more sparkle than the bluest water.

"You live here? Alone?"

"Yes, I live here, but no, not alone. There are others. Our house is on the other side of the island, but I come over here because of the shells. I like to think of this as my own private beach." He grinned and led the way around the cove to where a stream flowed out of the trees and over the sand into the waves. "There's a waterfall up there and a path next to it. If you follow the path, you come to my home. That route takes a while, though, so I prefer to follow the stream." He stepped into it, and so did Garrett, the cool water a contrast to the warmer Caribbean. "It comes from the rain and flows down the hill." Nigel sat on the sand, drawing his knees upward. "Where did you come from?"

"Originally Baltimore. I rented the boat in Barbados." Garrett sat down as well. "Do you like it on the island?"

Nigel shrugged. "This is the only home I've ever really known."

That shocked Garrett a little. Nigel had to be twenty-two or so. What kind of life had he experienced if he'd spent much of it on a lonely island? "Who else is here?"

"My aunt and brother, as well as Fairfield. He's sort of our caretaker and helps us all with anything we need. There's also a small village on the far side of the island with about fifty people, I guess. Fairfield has a boat that he can take to other islands, but he always goes alone."

That sent Garrett's curiosity through the roof.

"Fairfield says there's nothing there but greedy people, and he's always happy to be back. Jules and I spend our time together mostly. Jules is my brother." Nigel smiled again. There didn't seem to be an ounce of guile in this guy, and yet what he said made no sense. Why hadn't he ever wanted to get off this island? And what kind of aunt keeps her nephews cooped up? Still, it wasn't any of his business.

"Do you come to this side of the island often?" Garrett asked, absently digging his hands in the sand, letting it sift through his fingers, because who in the hell wouldn't want to be close to this magnetically attractive man? The way Nigel looked at him was intriguing, and Garrett wanted to be looked at by Nigel for as long as humanly possible.

"It's great swimming over here, and I can dive for shells. I collect them." Nigel seemed so pleased.

"Where do you keep this collection?"

Nigel pointed. "Out there. I find them and make sure they're okay, but I keep the collection in the water. They aren't really mine, of course. They belong to themselves, just like I do, but I keep an eye on them." He jumped to his feet before Garrett had a chance to think too much about that. "Wanna see?" He was already walking toward the water.

"I didn't bring a mask," Garrett said, wishing he had thought to grab snorkel gear before he'd dived off the boat, but it hadn't occurred to him that he would meet a man-god with a shell collection beneath the water.

Nigel tossed Garrett his. "I already know where they all are." He grinned and jumped into the water. Garrett put on the goggles and went in after him.

The bottom of the lagoon was covered in white sand, with coral rocks dotting the seascape, along with bits of seaweed. Shells rose up from the smooth bottom like hills, and when Garrett surfaced, Nigel told him about each one. "That's Zeus, he's the oldest and biggest. Athena is nearby, along with Aphrodite and Poseidon." He demonstrated on his hands to show their positions. He laid out a map in the air, and when Garrett looked again, he saw each and every one. "Mercury and Perseus."

"What do you do with them?" Garrett asked. "Do you eventually eat them?" Conch was a delicacy in some places.

Nigel shook his head. "Not these. That's why I keep them here. My aunt likes conch chowder, so she would eat them if she found them, but I don't. So I bring them here to save them. Otherwise there would be none left."

Garrett treaded water as small waves rolled past. "Are they gone on the rest of the island?"

"No. But a lot less. I bring my friends here, and they have babies and make more friends that spread out. I'm the only one who comes here, so they're safe." He seemed proud of himself, and Garrett supposed Nigel had every right to be.

Nigel swam back to shore, and Garrett followed. They sat once again near the stream in the shade of a coconut palm. "How long will you be here?" Nigel asked after a few minutes of silence.

"I don't know. There's no place I need to be." God, it was peaceful. Tropical breezes blew through the trees, rustling the fronds, and Garrett would be happy to stay here forever. He sat up and tugged his shirt over his head before lying back down on the sand, then closed his eyes for a few minutes and just let himself be.

When he opened his eyes, he found Nigel looking at him, watching him, with naked desire in his eyes. It had been a long time since Garrett had seen that kind of unashamed longing without a hint of caution.

"You're a very handsome man," Nigel said softly.

"Thank you." Warmth spread through him at the admiration and heat radiating from Nigel. Damn, it was heady being admired and ogled like that. Not that Garrett intended to do anything. The last thing he wanted was to pop the bubble of an innocent, and all indications were that Nigel was as innocent as they came. "Do you have friends here?"

"Like Sancho Panza and Don Quixote? No. There is no one here to be friends with like that." Nigel turned away, staring out to sea. "There is just Jules and me. He is my friend and also my brother, but it's not the same."

"No, I suppose not," Garrett said as a bell rang somewhere, the sound carried on the wind.

"I have to go." Nigel jumped to his feet. "I'll be back. Will you stay?" He was already heading toward the break in the trees that formed the path.

"Yes. I can stay for a few days," Garrett agreed. This was as quiet a place as any, and the view was spectacular.

"Okay. I will be back later." Nigel waved and disappeared down the path.

Garrett watched him go, blinking a few times. With Nigel gone, the only indication he'd been there at all were his footprints in the sand, and many of those were already disappearing in the tide. This whole encounter could have been part of his imagination if it wasn't for the lingering heat that stayed behind, and the small pile of shells near the edge of the beach that Nigel had been gathering when he'd first arrived.

Garrett got up, grabbed his shirt, and pulled it back on before walking into the waves, swimming back to the boat, and climbing on board once again. He changed into dry clothes and hung the wet ones out, then went inside to get something to eat. He sat topside in the shade and found himself watching the path just in case Nigel returned. Garrett barely tasted his food or paid attention to what he did. A gull actually snapped the last bite of bread from off his plate. Not that he cared.

He wondered when Nigel would return and hoped it would be soon. He kept peering out the small windows to see if his visitor had returned. But he didn't… and Garrett continued to watch.

CHAPTER 3

GARRETT WATCHED for Nigel for much of the afternoon, beating himself up the entire time. On one hand, he wanted Nigel to return so he could see him again. Yet part of him hated how much he wanted to see Nigel, because it felt like he was giving up some of David, and he wasn't ready to do that. Every day he felt David drifting farther and farther away, his memories growing rounder and less sharp, so he held on to them as hard as he could. Garrett hadn't longed for a man since he'd met David. And he certainly hadn't sat on a boat, or anywhere else, watching and waiting for someone to appear.

When he wasn't looking for Nigel, Garrett debated pulling up anchor and getting the hell out of there. It would be best if he simply left, putting nautical miles between him and Nigel so he could hold on to his memories and nothing important would change.

Garrett closed the book he'd been trying to read for the past two hours, because the words swam on the page and his thoughts kept pulling him elsewhere. If he'd been on land, he'd have paced the room, but there was no space on the boat for that, so he dropped the book onto one of the deck seats and lay back with a groan.

Another bell sounded on the breeze, and once again Garrett wondered what they meant. Maybe they were a simple way of letting the people on the island know that dinner was ready? Or did they mean something more ominous? Garrett's stomach rumbled, so he heated up a can of soup and made a sandwich, then sat on deck as he ate, lying to himself that he wasn't watching for Nigel.

Garrett swallowed the last of his soup, carefully did the dishes to preserve water, and put them away. When he returned to the deck, Nigel stood on the beach, waving.

Garrett thought about turning and going back inside, but his heart sped up and he couldn't stop looking. Nigel wore a pair of blue board shorts and a tank top that, even from this distance, Garrett could tell fit him like a glove. Garrett changed quickly, made sure everything was secure, dropped the ladder in the water, and made the swim to shore.

"You stayed," Nigel said. "I was afraid you would be gone or that you were like the people in my books who only exist in the story or in my mind."

Garrett chuckled, as he'd thought something very similar. "I'm real." And if that was true, then Nigel was real as well. "Did you have a good day? I read a while and took a nap through the afternoon heat."

Nigel shrugged. "It was normal. Though Jules found a turtle nest, and he's watching it to make sure it isn't disturbed. Some of the birds and lizards on the island will eat the eggs, and we want them to hatch so we can watch the little turtles scamper into the sea." He laughed innocently. "It will take some days before they hatch, so Jules put a cage around the nest to protect it. He'll take it off when hatching gets closer."

"Did he see the turtle lay the eggs?" Garrett sat on the cooling sand. His gaze wandered up Nigel's lightly furred legs and then his strong, lanky body.

Nigel plopped down next to him, stretched out his long legs, and propped himself up with his forearms. "Yes. We watched her from one of the windows in the house. It was evening, and as soon as she covered up the eggs and left, we went down to protect them. Now Jules watches them all the time, like he's their mother."

"How long ago was that?" Garrett wanted to hear Nigel talk, especially about something that clearly excited him.

"She laid the eggs about seven weeks ago, and we check on them all the time but don't disturb them. They should hatch in a week to ten days." Nigel clapped his hands together once. "Maybe you could stay and watch them hatch too! It will be so exciting. The babies will dig their way out of the nest and then scurry to the sea. It will be cool if they all make it to the water and some survive. That way they'll come back here to lay their eggs sometime in the future."

"Does that happen often?" Garrett found himself interested even if he'd never given the nesting habits of sea turtles a second thought.

"Turtles return to where they were born to lay their eggs, so some must have at some point. It could be that she got blown off course and had to lay her eggs here, though. I don't know." Nigel rocked slightly in his excitement, and Garrett tried to imagine a world where something like hatching sea turtle eggs could make someone so excited.

"You must love it here," Garrett said.

"I do. There's so much. This cove has my conches, and they will grow and be happy and make more conches. There's the sea turtle nest beach, and around that way are rocks, and the shore is rough where the waves come in off the ocean and scour the island. There's a blowhole over there, and when the tide is up, it shoots water high in the air. Sometimes I like to go watch it. Then there are the birds and lizards. We see them all the time. They stay because there's plenty of food for them." Nigel bounced slightly, rocking on his heels. "What about where you live? What's it like?"

"Baltimore is a big city. Really big."

"Bigger than this island?" Nigel asked, like such a thing was absurd. It took Garrett a beat to comprehend that this little place truly was Nigel's whole world.

"Yes. Probably ten times bigger. It has buildings clad in glass windows that go hundreds of feet into the sky, and huge restaurants and shopping centers all connected by roads and freeways." Garrett tried to think of a way to describe a city to someone who had never seen one. "It's built around the harbor, with large boats, and it even has an aquarium with ocean life from around the world, including a few sea turtles."

Nigel looked at him like he was from outer space. "Do people live in those big buildings? How do they get up there? If they walk, they must be tired before they get to the top. So many stairs."

Garrett didn't laugh. "They have elevators that take you all the way up. They use engines to pull you up with cables."

"Oh yeah, I remember them now. Wouldn't it be great if they went sideways like in Harry Potter? Do they have handholds and go sideways?" The gleam in his eyes was magical.

"No. They just go up and down." As soon as Garrett said it, he realized Nigel was joking.

Nigel looked at him with just a hint of a wry grin. "Still, that would be fun to go up that high. I bet you can see forever from up there. I sometimes go to the top of the house so I can watch ships pass on the horizon."

"You can look out over the entire city as it spreads out from downtown, out to where people live. It's pretty big." Garrett sat back. "But not as nice as this. There are people everywhere, and lots of noise from cars and buses, lights from signs and buildings. It doesn't really get super dark anymore because of all the light, and you can only see the brightest stars at night." It occurred to him that at home, he probably wouldn't be able to see the star he had picked for David.

Nigel tilted his head to the side as he watched him. "Why are you sad? Is it because you have to go back to the city and leave this beautiful island? I wonder what it must be like out there, but then I wouldn't be here, and this is my home."

Garrett tried to imagine a life where he didn't know about the outside world, its turmoil and stress. Hell, what must it be like to live where the most exciting thing was a clutch of turtle eggs and the biggest threat was a storm that blows in off the ocean? Where everything was tropical and perfect and there were no guns, no people selling drugs and each other… just an ideal place with ideal weather and turtles and conches and birds and lizards?

A coconut *thunk*ed to the sand nearby, and Nigel picked it up, shook it, and then smiled. He ran back to the edge of the woods, pulled out a huge machete, and lopped off the top until he'd made a hole to the center.

"Drink this," he said, handing the coconut to Garrett. "Just tip it up slowly."

Garrett did as instructed, and liquid poured out onto his tongue. It was close to coconut water but had a definite flavor. Once it was empty, Nigel split open the coconut, dug out some of the flesh, and handed it to him. It tasted nothing like what he bought in the store, and Garrett ate the entire piece.

"It's really good."

"I like it. The trick is to wait for them to fall on their own. Some people climb up to get them, but then they might not be ripe. If it falls on its own, then it's probably ready." Nigel plopped back down, eating some of the coconut himself. "I bet you can't do that in the city."

"No. Though you can buy coconut at the store." Garrett wondered why he was defensive about living in the city. It wasn't as though he had decided that it was city living or Baltimore in particular that was the end-all, be-all of... well, anything.

"What else is there fun to do where you live?"

"When I was a kid, we used to go fishing or crabbing. Maryland is famous for a particular type of crab, and we used to catch those off the dock. My dad used to take me and my sister sailing. That was where I learned to navigate and spend time on the water. What about your dad?"

Nigel shrugged. "I don't have one. My mom and dad died when I was a kid. I remember them a little, but Dad was always working, and Mom stayed home but was really busy. I spent a lot of time with a nanny. After they died, Jules and I came to live here with my aunt."

He made it sound so simple, like everyone came to their own tropical island after their parents died. But Garrett supposed if this was all he knew and understood, there were definitely worse places to grow up, even if it was isolated.

Nigel looked around as though uncomfortable. "Do you want to see the waterfall? It's up that path about ten minutes. There's a deep spot near there where I like to swim." He looked down. "Are those the only shoes you have? They aren't very good for hiking."

"They're my water shoes." With the coral on the seabed, he'd figured it was best if he wore shoes. "It will be okay as long as we don't walk too fast." Garrett got up and followed Nigel into the dense tropical foliage, keeping to the path until it made a bend, and sure enough, a waterfall tumbled down the rocks, ending up in a pool about forty feet across.

Nigel stepped down and slid into the water. "It gets deep fast, but it's cool." He paddled out near a twenty-foot waterfall.

Garrett pulled off his shirt and stepped into the pool. It was dang near cold, but in the almost ninety-degree heat, it felt amazing. He swam over to Nigel, who waited with a smile.

"You can get under the waterfall, but you probably don't want to. Jules is a real good swimmer and he gets pushed down. I just let the spray get my head wet and stuff." He floated on his back, and Garrett did the same, looking up at the water as it cascaded over the ledge and began its downward plunge. There was something almost hypnotizing about the motion, the sun catching droplets, making them sparkle.

"It's really beautiful." Perfection in paradise was a much better description, but Garrett had never been a poet, and the scene in front of him deserved more words than he could find, so he just looked at the view and tried to be happy.

"Hey," Garrett sputtered after a wall of water washed over him. He swam to the side and splashed Nigel back. "Think that's funny?" Garrett was soon dripping as water ran off him. The amount that Nigel managed to splash left him wondering if he'd emptied the pool.

Garrett laughed, deep and pure from the depths of his soul, and Nigel did the same, the happiness bouncing off the rock walls. It felt so damned good, and yet, when Garrett heard himself, a stab of guilt struck his gut for a second before it was gone. David would want him to be happy again.

Nigel suddenly stopped, and Garrett realized he'd been standing there without moving. He didn't want to talk about it, so he grinned and splashed as big as he could.

"Sneaky." Nigel laughed and returned fire until they were both dripping and so was the shirt Garrett had set aside.

"I give," Garrett said, stepping out of the pool into the shade, still chuckling. Nigel stopped and did the same.

Nigel's tank was plastered to his chest, transparent, his nipples peaked and showing through. Garrett probably took too long looking, because Nigel glanced down and then up again, and smiled. "You are very handsome," Nigel said without changing expression, as though complimenting a man he'd just met was commonplace. Maybe in his perfect world, it was.

Garrett smiled. Nothing in his experience or training had prepared him for this situation. He and David had circled each other for a while, doing a short dance of uncertainty and angst.

Nigel tugged off his shirt, and Garrett got a close-up look at a flat belly and a lanky body built through years of sun, outdoors, and good living. He was as beautiful a man as Garrett had ever seen. Nigel dropped his shirt and for a minute stared openly at Garrett, whose first instinct was to cover up under such a naked appraisal.

"You're really strong, I bet." Nigel took a step closer. "How do you get big muscles like that?" He actually reached out to touch Garrett's arm, sending a ripple of heat radiating throughout his body.

"In the city, we have gyms where we lift weights. In my job, I have to be strong." Garrett didn't pump or show off, but he couldn't help bending his arm just a little. "You...."

"I don't have a gym."

Garrett nodded. "You don't need one." Nigel was perfect just the way he was. Garrett felt excitement building and hoped it didn't show. "You have the waterfall and the ocean, and the footpaths you walk on and the beaches where turtles lay their eggs. People go to the gym because, in the city, they don't have those kinds of things."

"Oh." Nigel looked down again and then at Garrett. "I don't look like you...." He continued examining Garrett with no shyness at all. "I like the muscles." There wasn't the barest hint of coloration on his cheeks, like he didn't know that most people would be embarrassed by saying something like that. "I read a book once—Aunt Phyllis didn't know it was in a stack of books she gave me. It's called *Maurice*, and Maurice likes boys instead of girls. It was a long and very depressing book. I didn't like it very much." He made a precious face, like he'd eaten a bad coconut.

"What did you think of the situation?" Garrett had seen the movie some time ago with David. He had to admit, the film was beautiful but depressing for the most part.

"It made me think. Is it really bad for boys to like other boys like that?" Nigel locked his gaze onto Garrett's with a pleading sort of desperation that lasted only a few seconds. "I think it was a long time ago," he added with a shrug.

"No. It's not bad." Garrett didn't mention that he was gay because he didn't want to lead Nigel to any sort of conclusion. And at that moment, a little distance between them might be a good thing, because he had no idea how much longer he was going to be able to control himself. Nigel stood so close, his fingers still caressing his arm, his little pink tongue caressing perfect lips, and those eyes—blue as the invitingly warm water and even more beckoning.

"Oh. Good." Nigel came to stand toe to toe with Garrett, then leaned even nearer. The kiss, when it happened, was a little clumsy, but as sweet and gentle as the caress of a summer breeze. Nigel almost jumped back in what Garrett hoped was surprise, grinning as he touched his lips. "You kiss good."

It took a moment to register that he had been kissed, and not by David. Guilt welled up, and Garrett had to remind himself that it was okay to move on. His head understood that easily enough, but his heart needed convincing.

Nigel stood there expectantly, and Garrett forced himself to swallow his guilt, then smiled and nodded.

"We can kiss again." It wasn't a question, and within seconds, his arms were filled with wet, wriggling Nigel, who seemed to have turned into the Energizer Bunny, which added to Garrett's building excitement. This time he kissed with building heat and intensity that shredded any of Garrett's remaining reluctance. Nigel was a fast learner, or Garrett's superpower was teaching innocent, twenty-two-year-old horny boys how to kiss. Either way… holy cow.

Garrett broke the kiss, swallowing and gaping in complete surprise. "I bet you didn't learn to do that from your books."

"*Lady Chatterly's Lover*," Nigel said. "It was in one of those boxes too. Granted, it had girls in it, but I thought the basic concept would be the same." He grinned. "It turns out I was right." He practically giggled. "I know what people do together. I'm not some ignorant, island-living kid. I read. It's just that I've never gotten to try anything out on a real live person before. I kissed my aunt a few times, but that was on the cheek and really different."

Garrett figured he'd play along. "How so?"

Nigel clearly wasn't expecting the question. "You don't know?" He widened his eyes and then caught on. "Silly... there were no tingles when she did it."

"And there were with me?" Garrett asked, swallowing hard because he wanted there to be more than anything.

Nigel bit his lower lip. "Yes. Did you not feel them? Maybe I did something wrong." He put his hand over his mouth, cheeks reddening. "Am I a bad kisser? Do I kiss like a fish?" he asked seriously.

"No. You don't kiss like a fish, and yes, I felt the tingles too." Garrett sighed, glad Nigel had as well. "And to answer your next question, no, it doesn't always feel like that. At least it doesn't for me." And part of him wished it hadn't this time. Then it would be so easy to sail away and not look back.

"Oh, so it's good, then." Nigel stepped closer, and Garrett gently put his hands on Nigel's shoulders.

"There is a lot more to... well, tingles... than just kissing." He needed to get his head screwed on straight before he did something he might regret, like seeing what the rest of Nigel tasted like. His mind flooded with images and the imagined taste of Nigel's skin as he rolled his tongue around one of his perky nipples or swirled it into his perfect innie.

"Like what?" Nigel put his hands on his hips, expression firm.

"Well, if you read books, you know that people talk and they find out about each other. Some people go right to kissing and then on to other things, but that's lust." And Garrett was not going to take advantage of Nigel's innocence like that. He knew very well what that felt like, and no one deserved that kind of experience. "It's best if you get to know the other person. Find out what they like, where they come from, what sort of things they like to read, foods they like, movies they enjoy. Make sure you have things in common, besides kissing and—" He swallowed. "—other things."

"Like sex." Nigel rolled his eyes, and Garrett had to stop himself from chuckling. "I know what sex is. I've seen the animals do it. I'm not an innocent."

But he was in many ways, and that was part of what was scaring Garrett half to death.

Garrett sat on the rock at the edge of the pool, watching the cascading water. "There's knowing about sex and then knowing what sex can mean, especially when you love someone. Sex and love mixed is very different and really special. Much better than sex alone." He could barely believe they were having this conversation. He'd just met the guy yesterday. Garrett tried to think of a time when he'd ever just met someone and had such a personal conversation right off the bat. Of course, the people he met hadn't grown up on an island away from all other people. Nigel didn't have all the preconceived notions of how he should behave derived from the wider world. All those things that everyone learned from the other kids—peer pressure, self-consciousness, teenage angst, the traumas of middle school and high school—all of those were probably missing for him.

Nigel carefully sat down next to him. He was clearly confused and watched Garrett as though he were speaking another language. "Why not just follow what you want? If I want to have sex, and you want to have sex… then why can't we just have sex? If it feels good and makes us both happy, what's wrong with that?" His argument was completely logical—except Garrett knew sex wasn't just logic and fun, at least for him.

"Because there's more than that." He sighed and stared at the water, unable to look at Nigel. "I had someone in my life who meant very much to me. He was the other half of my soul. I met him in the seventh grade, and we were friends for a while until he moved away. I was seventeen then and thought my world would break into pieces. But, of course, it didn't." All the highs were so very high, and all the lows exaggerated to the very depths of hell. Sometimes he thought it was a miracle he'd survived being a teenager at all. No wonder his mother had gray hair. "I met him again when I was a little younger than you, and almost without me knowing it, he became the center of my world. I loved my job, but I adored him." Garrett closed his eyes, wondering why in the hell he was even talking about this. He dipped his hands in the water, splashing into the pool just to do something to keep them from shaking. "He was at a business dinner with a client and on his way home. It was late at night, and a kid who barely had his license… he was drunk…. They hit so hard… the cars—they caught fire…." That was the day that Garrett's happiness died, the day he stopped living, and after the funeral and the interment, he'd buried himself in his job. Garrett still wasn't sure he was ready to rejoin the living.

"So, when you think about having sex, you think of him…?" Nigel kicked his feet. "I can understand that… I think. My books are full of stories about people who still hurt for a long time after someone dies. Like it doesn't really heal. It's a common theme. I always wondered if it was true or if it was a storytelling device."

"Losing him was like losing a part of myself and knowing I was never going to get it back." Garrett smacked the water, sending spray shooting everywhere.

"I'm sorry," Nigel said softly.

"You said you lost your parents. Do you remember how that felt?" Garrett didn't dare turn or he'd lose the tenuous hold that was keeping him from breaking down. And, dammit, he'd worked and held himself together for a year now.

"Yes. I was young, but I remember the funeral and holding Jules's hand as he cried. We had to be strong, so I waited to cry until I was alone. Then my aunt said that she was going to take care of us and that we'd have a nice house in an amazing place. She brought us here, and we've been on this island ever since." Nigel smiled. "It's nice here, and we have everything he and I could need." He jumped to his feet. "I know everything about this island. Stuff that Aunt Phyllis and Fairfield don't know about. Like the cave up in that hill, or that there's another little stream that runs over there." He pointed. "I've been everywhere on this island, and so has Jules. Even to the village."

"So you don't bring your aunt along with you all the time?"

Nigel shook his head. "Aunt Phyllis likes the inside. She cooks and stuff like that, but she doesn't like to leave the property." He finally blushed over something. "She hates snakes, and Jules loves to tease her and tell her stories about the ones that are on the island." Nigel grinned something fierce. "There are no snakes here at all. Some lizards, but not snakes."

"What is the village like? Can I get some supplies there?" Garrett asked. "Maybe you could take me."

Nigel's expression clouded over for a second, and Garrett reevaluated his analysis. Maybe Nigel wasn't as guileless as he'd originally thought. "I could, but Fairfield and Aunt Phyllis would get angry if I did. Aunt Phyllis and the village leader don't get along at all. The only part of the island she doesn't own is the area around the village, and she wants to buy it." Nigel shook his head. "I know she wants to put them off the island. She told me so once. But I don't want her to. They're nice people who are trying to live a quiet life. Sometimes I see them when I'm out camping and stuff." Nigel colored, and the shade of red on his cheeks was adorable. "I used to watch one of the boys in the village...."

The bell rang, carried by the wind.

"I should go."

"What is that?"

"Just Fairfield. He rings the bell to tell us it's time for dinner. He knows that Jules or I can be all over the island, so he doesn't try to call us. If we're late, then we have to get our own food." Nigel shrugged. "Like that's such a big deal." He pulled on his shirt. "Do you know how to get back to your beach?"

"Just down that trail?" Garrett pointed, and Nigel nodded, taking his first steps toward the jungle.

"I have to go, but I'll come to see you as soon as I can get away again." He hurried down the trail, leaving Garrett wondering as he watched him go. Was Nigel sneaking off to see him? And why would he feel the need to sneak away?

"I'll stay a while longer," Garrett agreed with a nod.

Nigel waved and smiled before turning back around and disappearing into the dense undergrowth. Garrett pulled his shirt over his head, getting the clingy fabric down his back, and then rinsed a pebble out of his water shoes before heading down the path, turning to look at where Nigel had disappeared.

Garrett reached the beach and sat on a piece of driftwood stuck in the sand. Something wasn't quite right. Nigel lived on this beautiful island with an aunt and a caretaker. That was unusual to say the least. Where had they gotten the money to live and to buy the island? It wasn't likely that they lived strictly off what the island could produce, and Nigel had said that this Fairfield guy periodically went for supplies, yet Nigel and Jules never went along or got off the island. What the hell was going on here, and why did Nigel allude to the fact that he had to sneak away? As the old saying went, something definitely smelled fishy.

The waves lapped at the beach, and Garrett looked out at his boat, which suddenly seemed exposed. To what, he wasn't sure. But his gut told him there was something off, and he needed to try to figure out what that was. Maybe Nigel was in some sort of trouble.

Garrett thought about going back to the boat, pulling up anchor, and sailing around the island to get a look at the rest of it, but then thought the better of it. If something suspicious was going on, why tip his hand? No one except Nigel seemed to know he was here, and if that was true, Garrett wanted to keep it that way. He figured he'd stay until Nigel returned and then would follow him back to the house and scope things out for himself.

With a course of action set, he walked into the water and swam back to the boat to wait for Nigel's return.

CHAPTER 4

THE BELL rang again, and after a little while, as the sky reddened and the clouds blazed with color, Nigel appeared on the beach. He waved, and Garrett waved back. Not up for swimming this time, he climbed into the small inflatable dinghy and rowed the short distance to shore.

"I came back as soon as I could." Nigel hurried over to him and helped Garrett pull the boat up on shore before kissing him. The joy that radiated from Nigel took on a life of its own and carried Garrett right along with it.

"Are you sneaking away so you can come see me?" Garrett asked, stroking Nigel's cheek. So much for subtlety. His plans flew out the window as soon as he had Nigel in his arms.

Nigel glanced downward. There was no guile in him in the least. "Yes. Fairfield is very protective, and he keeps a watch on us. Jules nearly drowned last year when a current got hold of him. I was able to rescue him in my canoe, but Fairfield has been extra protective ever since. I think he takes it as his personal responsibility to keep us safe." Nigel blinked a few times. "But there are some things he doesn't need to know, and I like that I can have you all to myself. There are just the four of us and the villagers on the island, so we share just about everything. But I like that I don't have to share you. I can make believe that you're mine… at least for as long as you stay."

"Are Fairfield and your aunt married?" Garrett asked. "Or involved with each other?"

Nigel giggled and put his hand over his mouth. "Fairfield is too old."

"You know, people of different ages fall in love, especially when they've been together somewhere, like on an island, for a long time."

Nigel tilted his head slightly, like he'd never thought of the possibility. Then he shivered and rolled his eyes.

"I take it the idea is kind of disturbing."

"Like eating a rotten coconut." Nigel made a face, complete with scrunched-up eyes and his tongue sticking out. Garrett chuckled under his breath, trying with all his might not to think about that perfect pink tongue. "That's not tasty."

"I don't suppose it is." Garrett wanted to ask him more about his home and his aunt and caretaker, but Nigel took his hand and began tugging him up the beach toward an old rockfall, worn smooth by the waves, that made the northern boundary of the beach.

"Come on. It's fun to climb." Nigel scampered over, and Garrett followed.

The rockfall created a second, much smaller cove where the waves had carved the island back a good twenty feet and left a tidal pool. Even in the setting sun, Garrett could see marine life filling the pool, scooting away as they approached.

"Where are we going?" Garrett asked as Nigel continued forward, around the edge of the pool and then to the far edge of the jungle. A cave had been carved into a rock wall that went up twenty feet or so.

"The waves don't reach here anymore," Nigel said as he went inside. That might have been true, but Garrett wondered what else used the cave. It wasn't too deep, and he stepped around a small firepit. "Be right back." Nigel hurried away and returned with an armload of sticks and dry leaves that he used to make a small fire. "Are you hungry? I can get some food. Just feed the sticks into the fire." Then Nigel was gone, and Garrett sat alone in the cave with a crackling fire.

Part of him, the skeptical and self-preservation pieces of his personality, wondered if Nigel had brought him here as a setup. That had to be the stupidest notion Garrett had ever had, but still… as darkness closed in around the mouth of the cave, it became pretty clear that he wasn't going anywhere tonight. Sure, he could follow the water back to the old rockfall, but getting over it while not being able to see would be impossible.

He shivered in the warm night air, wondering just what he'd allowed himself to get mixed up in. Part of him said that, curiosity be damned, he should pack up and get the hell out of here just as soon as it got light. This island, and Nigel in particular, was fraught with pitfalls. And Garrett still needed to somehow come to grips with the fact that David was gone and determine how he was going to live without him.

Garrett stared into the open flames as memories danced across his mind like the light from the flames waltzed on the walls of the cave. David loved camping and sitting around the campfire. Really, he just liked making out in the firelight, be it at a B and B, a campground, or in the middle of the woods. If Garrett built a fire, within ten minutes, David's eyes would have been glossed over and he'd turn to him, lean in close, and the necking would be on. More than once, when they were in a tent, Garrett had had to silence David, because, man, he was a sound machine during sex—the pushiest bottom in the history of gaydom. Garrett smiled to himself and let the memories run their course.

David had been the antidote to the ugly and inhumane world Garrett encountered in his job. Without David, there was nothing to counter the work, so it had taken over. He loved his job, but he'd escaped into it. If he was busy and tired as shit, he couldn't think about what was missing. Now, out here, smack-dab in the middle of nowhere, he had nothing but time to think and—

"I found some papaya and mango," Nigel said. "I love these." He plopped down next to Garrett and pulled a small folding knife out of his pocket, peeled the fruit, and cut off pieces. "Aunt Phyllis makes this amazing dessert—she calls it Magic Mango Mousse. Jules and I love it." Nigel lifted a slice of mango, and Garrett found himself watching Nigel's fingers, a little mesmerized by the delicate way they moved. He absently opened his mouth, and Nigel slipped a slice of mango past his lips. He chewed and swallowed the tangy sweetness. Nigel was ready with another piece, and Garrett took the offered bite. "I personally like mango better than papaya."

They finished the fruit, and Nigel stepped to the mouth of the cave and tossed the peels and stuff into the water. Then he returned and started preparing the papaya. Garrett had to agree—he liked the mango better himself, but papaya was good too.

"What is this place?"

"My cave," Nigel answered with a grin. "I think, before the rockfall, the waves came all the way up here, but the fall changed the pattern and this filled with sand, creating the pool and leaving the cave dry. It must have happened a long time ago, though."

"Let me guess—this library of yours has books on geology."

"I have books on lots of things. I like books. Jules likes the ocean even more than me. That's why he was almost pulled away. He was following a small octopus, trying to get a better look at it, and got caught in the current. He knows nearly every square inch of the sea floor and all the creatures of the island. He's like Tarzan, except under the water. I swear sometimes he can talk to them. Most of the time they don't seem afraid of him either. It's really quite interesting."

Nigel finished feeding him the last of the fruit, watching intensely as Garrett chewed, and Garrett found himself watching as well. Their gazes shifted momentarily to the fire and then back to each other. Garrett didn't dare move as anticipatory tension built between them. A steady thump sounded in his ears and his stomach fluttered. In those few seconds, he pushed away the memories of the last time that had happened and just went with it.

Nigel leaned forward, tugging at Garrett with an invisible thread until he was doing the same. If Nigel had said a single word, Garrett probably would have pulled back. But Nigel just looked and moved closer, as though waiting Garrett out, the touch of flint in his eyes daring Garrett to pull away.

Nigel kissed him first, and almost immediately, Garrett wound his arms around Nigel, pulling Nigel to him, deepening the kiss. The fire's heat paled in comparison to what raged between them. Garrett knew, somewhere in the depths of his mind, in some box buried deeply, that this wasn't a good idea, but every other cell in his body screamed out for Nigel's tender touch and the way he seemed to know just what Garrett wanted.

Nigel slipped a hand under Garrett's T-shirt, searched and found a nipple, and tweaked it just right, sending Garrett's head into high orbit.

"Yes…," he hissed softly, arching his back. If he closed his eyes, he could easily imagine it was David again. But he didn't. This wasn't David, and he wasn't going to disrespect Nigel.

"You stopped," Nigel said. "Do you think I'm this other-half-of-your-soul man? Do you imagine him instead of me?"

Garrett cupped Nigel's cheeks in his hands. "No. I know who's here with me." He drew Nigel closer once again, looking deeply into Nigel's eyes. "I know where I am." He closed the distance between them, pressing Nigel back onto the sand. This wasn't the greatest place to do this sort of thing, but he wasn't going to stop now.

The kisses grew even more heated. Garrett tugged at the hem of Nigel's shirt and drew it upward, exposing his belly and chest to the warm glow of the firelight. "Beautiful," he hummed as Nigel groaned and vibrated under him. "You're wonderful."

Nigel shook, and Garrett had a pretty good idea what was going on. He remembered being young and so full of energy. Nigel's cries grew more urgent as Garrett slid his hand into the pair of loose shorts Nigel wore. He opened them and parted the fabric, exposing Nigel's cock to the air, then slid his hand up and down his length.

Nigel shook even more. "Please… yes… no…. It's too soon… oh God." Nigel shook hard, and Garrett knew his release was just seconds away. He locked gazes with Nigel, determined to see him through his experience. He gripped tighter, and Nigel tumbled over the edge, coming over Garrett's hand and onto his own belly.

For a few seconds, Nigel stared at him, wide-eyed, smiling blissfully. "Is that how it always is?" He heaved for breath, still grinning like he'd just been given the keys to the cooler that held the world's supply of ice cream.

"It all depends on how you feel and what you think." Garrett held still, his own excitement burning brightly, but right now, this moment between them had to be about Nigel. If this truly was his first time, then it had to be special, and Garrett's own release was less important.

"It was amazing." Nigel grinned, then sat up and kissed him hard. "You're amazing too." Somehow Garrett thought he was much less so, but he didn't argue. Garrett hadn't been amazing at any point in his life until he'd met David… and even then, the realization of exactly what David was to him had happened over time. This… whatever this was… with Nigel was like a freight train out of control, racing toward him, and he wasn't able to stop it or get the hell out of the way. And somehow he knew it was either going to smash him into a million pieces or pick him up and take him along for the ride at a hundred miles an hour. It was exciting and frightening at the same time.

"You're—" Garrett was at a loss for words, though they weren't his forte anyway, especially when it came to expressing his feelings. "A live wire…."

"Is that good?" Nigel shifted slowly, putting himself back into his pants.

"Yeah. It's good. Sexy and exciting." Garrett smiled.

"Am I like the other man?"

"You mean David? No. You're very different from him." He sighed. "You don't have to compete with him or anyone."

Nigel put his hands on his hips, a glare shining in his eyes. "Right. There are three of us here right now: you, me, and him. I know he's here, because he came with you. He's in your mind no matter what. That isn't necessarily bad, but he's gone."

Garrett stifled a growl. "David was the other half of me. I'm just supposed to let him go and not think of him anymore? My mother keeps telling me that it's time to move on. One of the other officers even offered to set me up on a date." He clenched his fists and looked back toward the rockfall. Maybe it was time for him to go back to the boat and…. "Shit," he whispered under his breath. Garrett had never run away from a fight or a challenge in his life, and a twenty-two-year-old kid with eyes as beautiful as the sea, hair the color of gold, and everything any gay man on the planet would want, had him running scared. He made Garrett uncomfortable and got him thinking that maybe it really was time for him to get on with his life.

"You're supposed to think of him, but not live for him." Nigel turned toward the fire. "That's what Aunt Phyllis told me after the funeral. It was okay for us to remember and love our mom and dad, but we had to go ahead and learn to live without them. She said that was part of why she was going to bring us here."

Garrett clamped his eyes closed and tried to tamp down the flips in his belly, but they didn't settle, so he opened his eyes. Nigel sat nearby on the sand, watching the flames, the light glowing in his hair like a halo. Garrett had to remind himself that this wasn't the city and that not everyone had some ulterior motive for everything they did. Nigel seemed to be honest about what he wanted from Garrett.

"I think that's good advice," Garrett said softly as some of the tension flowed out of him and his belly finally stopped roiling. "I'll try."

Nigel jumped to his feet. "I'll be right back." He hurried out of the cave, out of sight, and returned in just a few minutes carrying something wrapped in a green plastic tarp. "I told Aunt Phyllis and Fairfield that I was going camping tonight. Jules is doing the same, but out near the turtle eggs so he can watch them. He won't get too close, but he wants to make sure they're okay." Nigel set down the bundle and unwrapped the plastic, folding it and placing it off to the side. It held a white canvas bag that he set down, opened, and pulled out an old blanket with a tear in one corner. He spread it on the sand and then got a second one. This was nicer and in one piece. He put that over the other blanket before setting the mostly empty bag on top of the tarp. "There's some rope in there that I can use to string up the tarp if I need to, but we don't need that tonight."

"Camping?" Garrett asked.

"Sure. I love to camp out. It drives Fairfield a little crazy, but he's gotten used to it, and as long as we promise not to go in the water, he's okay with it." Nigel sat down on the blanket, slipped off his shoes, and wiped the sand off his feet before putting them on the fabric. "It isn't like either of us can actually go very far. The island is only so big. But after Jules nearly drowned, he took away my canoe and he and Aunt Phyllis made new rules about going in the water." He held out his hand, and Garrett got to his feet, brushing himself off, and took the same precautions before sitting on the blanket. Nigel scooched next to him and put another piece of wood on the fire. He still had a pile of it.

"Do we have to keep the fire burning all night?"

"No. There is nothing that will bother us. You might wake up with a lizard hanging around, but they scamper away as soon as you move." Nigel took off his shirt and lay down. Garrett did the same, and Nigel slid right up behind him, arm slipping around Garrett's waist. It wasn't until then that Garrett realized he'd been seduced. Nigel had an honest, up-front, yet innocent way of getting what he wanted. And apparently he wanted Garrett.

"Have you had other people visit the island?" The fire settled into the depression in the sand, its light slowly dimming.

"Once, a while ago. Some people were having trouble with their boat. They drifted onto shore near the house. Fairfield went out and helped them, and then they left. I wanted to go down and help, but Aunt Phyllis played games with us in the house. She said that one of the men on the boat had been sick and that she didn't want us to get what he had. We're not exactly on anyone's vacation list, and Aunt Phyllis owns nearly the entire island. We are officially part of Martinique, but they leave us alone."

"So you've spent much of the last… what, I'm guessing… ten or eleven, maybe twelve years pretty much alone on this island? Has your aunt said why?" The cop in him was more than a little curious, but he also didn't want Nigel to think he was giving him the third degree. "It seems a little unusual." He kept his voice light, but Nigel hung on every word.

"I guess it might seem that way. Aunt Phyllis tells the story of how she spent her childhood down here on the island she inherited from my grandparents, and she says that after the death of our mom and dad, eleven years ago, she had had enough and wanted to find a place where she could raise Jules and me without the threat of us getting hurt. Fairfield has been with my family for nearly thirty years, so he came with her to help protect us." Nigel smiled. "I once asked him if he was a butler after reading about one in a book, and he said that he was that and a lot more."

"Do you like him?" Garrett asked.

"Questions, questions," Nigel said. "Of course I like him. If I didn't, I think Aunt Phyllis would send him off the island. We all get along pretty well, I guess." He sighed softly. "What are things like with your family?"

"My mom and dad live in a house they built outside Baltimore a few years ago. Dad will retire in the next five years, and then he and Mom want to move to Florida. My mother has always had people to clean up after her. My grandfather started a clothing business in Baltimore. He sold it thirty years ago for a lot of money, so my mom doesn't quite get the concept of picking up after herself." Garrett shifted nervously. His relationship with his parents was complicated, very much so, and it was hard for him to describe.

"Fairfield and Aunt Phyllis never pick up after either Jules or me. We have to do our chores and keep our rooms clean."

"I love my mom and my dad, but they didn't understand when I told them I was gay." Garrett watched the fire as he spoke. "They thought it was a phase... something I would grow out of."

"But you didn't," Nigel said. "I used to wonder if it would change for me. I never talked to Aunt Phyllis or Fairfield about it. It didn't seem like it was any of their business. Did things change for you?"

"Mom and Dad loved David. I think he helped them see that I could have a full life. He was one of those people who is able to disarm anyone's argument with a smile. The first time he met my mother, he kissed her hand and charmed her. When he and I got married, my mom and dad were there, and they miss him too." Garrett rolled away from the fire to face Nigel. "But David is gone. Things with my folks are tough right now. I guess I didn't realize how much of the relationship we had as adults was because of him." So many of the good things in his life had been because of David. "I'm sorry. I need to stop talking about him all the time."

"I think I might have liked him."

Garrett laughed. He couldn't help it. "You and David probably would never have met. David hated boats and would never have gotten on one for as long as it took to come here. My dad used to sail, and he taught me and my sister. David once tried sailing for me and spent the entire day getting sick." God, he'd hated that sight. "I cut the sail short and just took him home."

"See, you're a good person too. It wasn't just him. He wanted to make you happy, and you took care of him when it didn't work out. It's what people who love each other do." Nigel held his gaze. "I bet you did things for him too."

Garrett nodded, but he was a little tired of talking about David. Usually, talking about him made his chest ache, but now, telling Nigel stories about David didn't hurt like that. "I did. He was easy to love. And I bet he would have liked you. If I could have gotten him here, he would have gone swimming, and he'd have loved to see your underwater collections." Garrett laughed. He could just see David and Nigel together. "When I went through his things, I found all his old collections… stamps, rocks, coins, baseball cards, Pokémon cards—you name it, he loved to collect it. They were all in boxes, carefully labeled and stored in the back of his closet." He sighed. "I think that's enough talk about our families. What else do you like to do besides read, camp out, and roam the island? Do you have television or the internet?"

"Not really. There isn't internet and no television stations, though Fairfield has a television and he plays movies on it sometimes that he gets when he goes out for supplies. But other than that, we don't watch stuff. There's so much to do outside and at the beach that Jules and I don't need to spend our time watching a screen with images of flat people on it. What do you like?"

"The Harry Potter movies," Garrett said.

Nigel perked right up. "They made the books into movies? I loved those stories. I think I would really like to see those."

Garrett wished he could make that desire come true, but he didn't have copies of the movies with him, and the internet connection from the boat was out of the question.

41

A breeze blew up off the water, swirling through the cave. It flickered the flames and then died away. It was so peaceful here, and whether he wanted it or not, that peace slipped into Garrett's spirit. Either that or it was Nigel.

"Garrett," Nigel whispered, drawing closer. "I don't want to talk anymore." His eyes shone in the firelight. "I feel like I'm being naughty, lying a little, being out here with you."

Nigel lifted the light blanket for them and shimmied underneath. Then he snuggled in again, tugging Garrett against him, holding him as he kissed forcefully. Garrett returned the kiss, winding his fingers through Nigel's soft hair, his other hand sliding down his back. He kept expecting to encounter fabric, but his hand slid over smooth skin to the small of his back, then over the curve of his butt. Garrett shivered with desire. Damn, Nigel certainly knew what he wanted and didn't have to say a word to get it. But that wasn't enough—*this* wasn't enough. Garrett needed to know that this was all right.

"Nigel," Garrett whispered as he stilled them both, rolling on his back, drawing Nigel on top of him. "Is this what you really want?" He cupped his butt, holding heaven in his hands.

"Yes," Nigel whispered.

"But why?" Things were moving really fast. Garrett could understand if Nigel was horny and just wanted to have sex. At his age, Garrett had most certainly been like that.

"You're a good man. You said no the first time I asked." Nigel put his hand over Garrett's chest. "I think you have a good heart."

"How do you know?" Nigel was way too trusting. "I'm here now, but you know I'm not going to be able to stay." And he doubted Nigel would be willing to run away with him. "I could just be interested in you for sex."

Nigel snorted. "Then why did you say no the first time and then tell me all that stuff by the waterfall?" He shook his head. "You are a good man and you care. I can tell."

Garrett waited for Nigel to make the next move. If this was what he really wanted, then Garrett wasn't going to argue.

Nigel leaned forward once again and took Garrett's lips in a kiss that seared all the way to his soul. He thought he'd had that part of him well secured, but Nigel seemed to have breached his defenses without much effort at all.

Nigel managed to get Garret's pants unfastened somehow. There was a lot of rolling and shifting, but they ended up on the sand at the edge of the blanket. Not that either of them cared. Nigel sighed as his entire body came in contact with Garrett's, found it as if he'd finally located something he'd been searching years for. Or maybe that was Garrett and he was just too scared to admit it. Either way, their kisses quickly grew frantic as they rocked and rubbed against each other.

Garrett squeezed Nigel's perfect firm butt, taking charge of their movements, because if he didn't, he was going to come within seconds. It had been years since he'd felt like a teenager, but Nigel had enough energy for them both and he sent it out in all directions, lighting up Garrett's mind with carefree passion. Garrett held on to Nigel and gave up control, letting him set the pace. Being with Nigel was like a recharge on his battered soul and spirit. He caressed up Nigel's back and across his shoulders, then up to his cheeks, holding them in his hands as he gazed into Nigel's shining eyes. "You're amazing, do you know that?"

"I like to think so," Nigel quipped back, and Garrett kissed the smirk off his face, turning his soft chuckle into a moan that went on for the longest time.

"You are. Somehow you touched my heart when I wasn't sure I wanted anyone to," Garrett whispered, letting the words fall away as pleasure—pure, basic, and wonderful—built inside him.

The fire sputtered and died, the last of the light fading away, leaving them in the darkness, just the two of them exploring and touching, one learning the joys of first love, and the other learning it was okay to love again. The ocean beat time, and their bodies picked up on it, heaving, flowing, until neither could control it any longer and their passion overwhelmed them.

Garrett held Nigel tightly, not wanting to let him go as lightness took over his heart. In the darkness, with Nigel still pressed to him, Garrett learned that his heart did indeed have room enough inside it for two, and if he wasn't careful, Nigel would take up residence.

CHAPTER 5

GARRETT WOKE to Nigel getting out of the blankets. He pretended to stay asleep just so he could watch Nigel's pert butt swing a little as he made his way to the far side of the clearing before stepping over some rocks. He returned a few minutes later and got back under the blanket. At least on the sand, he couldn't shake the mattress when climbing back in.

"I know you're awake. You breathe differently." Nigel settled, a warm hand sliding around Garrett's waist.

"You can't fault a guy for wanting to watch, can you?" Garrett grinned and held his breath as Nigel's hand wandered lower. "I didn't think so." He rolled over and tugged Nigel closer, then shifted until Nigel stared down at him. He loved this position, with Nigel's weight on top of him, his ass accessible for holding and grabbing. Nigel was already groaning as he ground his hips, sliding his cock alongside Garrett's. It shouldn't have been surprising that once Nigel got a taste of sex, he was raring to go. Not that Garrett wasn't also.

It was so simple, Garrett was almost shocked. He had never been an easygoing guy. But with Nigel it seemed to come naturally. He forgot about loss and pain, work, suspicions, and questions, and could just be, letting the moment take him. And damn, the moment turned into many strung together in a blissful, passionate circle that ran between him and Nigel. They both fed on it, enhancing it until it flowed back again, wilder, more powerful, until neither of them could hold out any longer. They cried out their passion, letting it hang in the air around them before being taken away, spread out on the breeze. Garrett held Nigel and fell back to sleep. He woke once again to Nigel slipping away.

45

"I have to go. Aunt Phyllis will worry if I am not back soon, and Fairfield will come out looking for me." He pulled on his clothes, and Garrett stretched and dressed as well.

Garrett helped Nigel fold away their campsite and cover the cold firepit with sand. Nigel kissed him hard, one thing led to another, and soon they were necking vigorously. Finally Nigel pulled away, said goodbye, climbed the rockfall, and disappeared from view. Garrett followed more slowly, taking advantage of a bush to do his business before using the small boat to paddle back to the sailboat.

He made a quick breakfast, thinking that, given Nigel's pattern, it wasn't likely he would be back until later in the day. So he hoisted the sails, hauled up the anchor, and headed for the other side of the island to see if the village had any of the supplies he needed.

IT FELT good to be out on the water, though it would have been nicer to have Nigel with him. They hadn't spent all that much time together, but Garrett still missed him. He even turned to the empty space next to him once, intending to ask a question, before he remembered he was alone.

The breeze freshened as he came out of the lee of the island, and he had to tack, turning into the wind a number of times to take advantage of the wind direction. Eventually Garrett saw the village near the shore and drew closer.

Ramshackle buildings—put together with wood, corrugated metal, and stone from the island—clustered together in a cove that faced north. The area seemed to provide a natural breakwater, and Garrett easily sailed into the bay, anchored offshore, and rowed the inflatable in.

A few people stopped to look and wonder, but most seemed busy and continued with their tasks. Old men worked with nets, while some women in bright clothes gathered under a tree, huddled near a cook fire, the spicy scent making his stomach rumble.

"Good morning," he said to a nearby man, hoping someone spoke English.

"Morning," the man said in a heavy accent that sounded vaguely French, but with surprising warmth.

"I needed some supplies, and I was told there was a small store here." Garrett looked toward the other side of the island, and the man nodded.

"Yes." He pointed. "Go there. They can help you," he said, his tone clipped now.

"Thank you," Garrett said lightly, ignoring the chill, and headed in the direction indicated. Inside the small building, he found shelves lined with canned food, dried food, snacks, and candy. Nothing perishable at all, which didn't surprise him. He did find a small stack of bottled water packs and took one to the counter.

A lady came in the door behind the counter and smiled, nodding as he added some Cheetos, because he was hungry for the damn things, as well as some cans of vegetables and fruit. She watched him and smiled as he finished gathering what he wanted. Then Garrett pulled out some US currency, and she nodded again, writing down his total.

"Thank you," he said politely.

"You welcome," she said, placing his purchases inside and handing Garrett a bag woven from palm fronds. He hefted the water and his other purchases, carried them to the dinghy, and placed them in the bottom. He wasn't in a hurry, so he wandered around.

"May I help you?" a man said as he caught up with Garrett.

"I've been on the boat for a while and thought I would stretch my legs before leaving. I sailed into a cove on the other side of the island and met Nigel, and he told me about the village here with a store. So I thought I'd get some supplies."

"I see," he said very levelly, and Garrett couldn't help noticing the tension. He wasn't sure if it was simply because of his presence there or if it had been the mention of Nigel. "Are you leaving soon?"

"The island seems pretty. I was going to sail around it." He smiled. "I'm Garrett, by the way." Garrett held out his hand.

"Mantu," he said, and shook it. "Sailing around is a bad idea. They not like it. Best to go and find another island to look at. You can

47

stay here, but they…." He turned away. "They really not like anyone else here on the island. We leave them alone and they let us be, but they strange people." He turned and walked away, leaving Garrett wishing he could ask him a few questions.

He wandered to the group of women, drawn by the scent coming from their fire. God, it smelled like a little spicy heaven, and he recognized the scent of Caribbean curry. One of the women patted dough flat and laid it on a griddle, like she was making a flatbread… no, more like a rustic crepe… of sorts.

"Do you like?" she asked with a gap-tooth smile.

"It smells wonderful."

"You come, taste." She pulled bread off the fire, filled it, and handed it to him. "Is roti."

He took a bite and hummed his pleasure.

"Is good?"

"Very good." The slight saltiness of the conch came through beautifully.

She motioned to a log, and Garrett sat down to finish the gift.

"You are a gifted cook." He smiled. "I'm Garrett."

"Maria." She laughed lightly. "You are flatterer." She waved her hand in his direction, laughing as she went back to her work. "You meet Mantu."

"Yes." Garrett hoped she'd continue to talk.

"He is leader. Good man. He not like…." Maria pointed inland. "They very different. Nigel and Jules, good boys, but rest." She shook her head.

"Nigel said that his aunt and the village didn't get along."

She continued working and looked both ways, probably for eavesdroppers. Clearly this lady liked to talk, and she seemed glad to have someone new to speak to. She was exactly the kind of person Garrett had been hoping to find.

He took another bite of the roti and nodded his approval. "I think I have a new favorite food."

Maria seemed pleased by that, and Garrett finished the snack. She glanced around her again. "Is what he tell you? She his aunt? You see her?" she asked, and Garrett shook his head. "She their aunt, and I barracuda." She flipped her head back and cackled out loud. "She no relation to boys. You look, you see."

"Oh, maybe I didn't understand him right."

"They think she aunt, but she not. There plenty strange things over there. We stay away." She moved her hands faster, as though she were agitated. "Boys come long time ago and never leave. The others, they leave, but never boys. That not right."

"Do you know why?" Garrett asked. "Nigel said it was because his aunt didn't want to leave."

"She definitely leave sometimes. I see. Boys stay and they not know she gone. They all over the island. We see them. They good boys. Others, I don't think so good." She grew quiet as Mantu and another approached.

Garrett figured it was time for him to be going and thanked her once again for the snack. He went to his boat, pushed it into the water, and waved goodbye to Mantu before heading to the sailboat. He loaded his supplies on board and secured the inflatable to the deck, then raised sail and the anchor before gliding out of the cove.

He stared out over the open water, steering the boat as he thought about what he'd been told. If Marie was right and Aunt Phyllis wasn't really Nigel and Jules's aunt, then who in the hell was she and why were they on this island? Did Nigel know she wasn't really his aunt and just called her that? Garrett discounted that almost immediately. Nigel's story about losing his parents and his aunt bringing him here had rung too true, and he stuck by his notion that there hadn't been any guile in Nigel. He had no reason to lie. So if that was the case, then that left the fact that Nigel and Jules were being deceived. Garrett shivered at the thought.

"What the hell is really going on?" he asked himself. Who were this aunt and caretaker who had kept Jules and Nigel on this island for all these years?

His natural police curiosity rose to the forefront as he steered back to the sheltered cove. He couldn't ask Nigel because it was likely he had no idea. Besides, what was he going to tell him? That his aunt wasn't his aunt, without a shred of proof? Nigel wasn't going to believe him. Hell, Garrett hardly believed what he'd walked into. No, he needed to keep this to himself and figure out what was going on just to try to keep Nigel safe. The thought of him being in jeopardy or hurt in any way only made him angry as hell.

Garrett gripped the wheel tightly, steering into the protected cove he'd come to think of as his and Nigel's, dropped the anchor, and lowered the sails. What he really needed was a plan, and Garrett sat under the sunshade with a notebook to try to piece together what he knew and his plan going forward.

GARRETT SAT there for much of the afternoon, trying to figure out how he should handle this. His mind went in circles. If what he'd been told was wrong, then Garrett should keep quiet and leave Nigel alone, and he could go on with his happy life. But if what he'd been told was true and Nigel knew…? If Nigel was aware of the truth, then regardless of how weird or unusual the situation was, he could make his own decisions. So, in both those cases, Garrett should keep his nose out of it and leave Nigel alone.

But… then what if what he'd been told was true and Nigel had no idea? Then the implication was that something nefarious was going on and, to some extent, Nigel was being held prisoner there on the island. And Nigel's innocence was being used against him. Every time Garrett's thoughts turned in that direction, he grew angry, and once he damn near tossed his notebook overboard out of sheer frustration.

He had to find out, and there was only one way he could think of to do that. Garrett needed to follow Nigel back to his house, get a look at it, and watch things to get some sort of lay of the land. There had to be a way to find out without Nigel knowing, so Garrett could get at the truth, one way or another. Then he could help.

Garrett actually thought of going to Martinique so he could find communication facilities and call back to the station for some advice, but his captain wouldn't be particularly happy if he knew he was getting involved with anything remotely resembling an investigation or police work. And the thought of leaving had Garrett's heart racing, and not in a good way. His guts twisted, instinct saying not to get too far away. Nigel was already too important to him to just let go and sail off for any damned reason.

But finding answers would mean some deception, and Garrett was conflicted over that. Nigel was so without guile. He was genuine and honest in a way that so little in Garrett's life was... and Garrett didn't want to taint that with lying. Nigel deserved the same in return. Hell, Garrett had already told him things he'd never told anyone else... ever. Nigel brought something out in him that made him want to open up and talk.

Garrett's ruminations continued for hours, with very little progress in any direction, except for one thing. He had to follow Nigel back to the house and watch.

As soon as Garrett made up his mind, as if by magic, Nigel stepped out of the undergrowth and waved from the beach. Garrett returned the wave, put together a bag of food, and paddled for shore. As he reached the beach, clouds thickened, blowing in off the sea, making Garrett glad he'd closed up everything on the boat.

Garrett drew the dinghy onto the sand, got out, and picked up the bag, and then they worked to secure the dinghy.

"We need to get over to the cave," Nigel said, watching the clouds draw closer to the water.

"Okay. I'll follow you." They hurried toward the rockfall and made it over and inside the overhang. Garrett set down the bag, and Nigel dashed out and returned with the camping bag just as the skies opened up.

The rain pummeled the ground and water, sending up a low-level roar that seemed to come from everywhere.

"This won't last too long."

"Are you sure?" Garrett peered out into a wall of water pounding the sand, worrying how bad this was going to get.

"Storms this time of year never last long. They come up, rain hard, and then go away. It's the nature of things." Nigel set the bag toward the back. "Don't worry. It's just some rain." He pulled out the ratty blanket and spread it on the ground. "I'll make a fire with the wood that's left from yesterday."

"There's some other wood, but it's all going to be wet."

"Get what you can, and we'll dry it off near the fire." Nigel grabbed the leftover wood as Garrett gathered what he could without getting drenched, dragging it under cover. "What did you do today?" Nigel asked as he worked.

"I got some supplies from the village." Garrett wasn't going to lie, but he didn't intend to tell the whole truth either. "They were nice enough, and it was a pleasant sail both ways. After that, I read and figured I'd plan what I wanted to do for the next couple of days."

"I see…." Nigel stopped feeding small branches in the fledgling flames. "And after that…?" His gaze locked with Garrett's, and Garrett had a hard time deciphering the depth in those blue eyes. There was hurt, but also something else that he couldn't place.

"Honestly, I don't know." Garrett swallowed. This island and the cove were supposed to have been a port in a storm, not a place for Garrett to stay forever. "All I can say is that I'll stay a few more days." It wasn't as though he wanted to hurt Nigel… not at all. So far, the plan was to see for himself that Nigel and, by extension, Jules were safe and then move on. That way he could leave without feeling like a complete heel. Was he going to leave a piece of his heart with Nigel when he went? Probably. But if he stayed around for too long, that piece was going to grow and then his heart would shatter again.

"Uh-huh." Nigel fed some more wood onto the fire. "I should have expected that, I guess." He turned away from Garrett, hiding his eyes—the first evasive thing Nigel had done since they'd met. Garrett wondered if he'd broken something fragile inside Nigel. "I thought you liked me."

Shit. "I do." Maybe he'd already stayed too long. Garrett had been worried about his own heart and getting hurt, but he knew the score and how things worked. He hadn't meant to, but it seemed he'd played with Nigel's heart. "But I came down here on vacation, and I will have to return home to my work." What did Nigel realistically expect?

"I know, I guess. It was stupid of me to think that... well... things could be different than that." Nigel set the wet wood around the fire to dry and stepped back, watching the flames without looking at Garrett.

The silence hurt more than if Nigel had yelled and gotten angry. Nigel had been open, talking, sharing, and giving of himself so freely since they met. Now he was guarded, and Garrett guessed that was something he was just starting to realize.

"I promise I won't leave without saying goodbye, and we can talk some more if you want."

Nigel nodded. "This is a nice place. It's always warm, and the wind always blows to keep things comfortable." He stood at the edge of the overhang, the rain pelting the sand just a foot from where he stood. "It rains sometimes, but the sun comes out too, and most everything you need is right here on the island."

Damn it all, Nigel was trying to convince him to stay.

Stick to what is practical and logical—that way the emotional quagmire that seems to be opening up in front of you can be held at bay and maybe, just maybe, avoided. "Your aunt and Fairfield don't know I'm here, do they? What would they think if they found out I was here and what we've been doing? I don't think they'd be happy, and it's doubtful I'm going to be welcome."

Nigel nodded, turning back to him. "You're right. They don't know about you or your boat, and they would be angry, or at the least disappointed in me." He bit his lower lip. "But is it wrong to want something... or someone... for myself? Everything here is shared— the house, the food. We all get what we need. But maybe I wanted something that was just mine. Is that so wrong?" The longing in his eyes was damn near frightening,

"No. We all need some things to be our own, to care for and to hold on to. I know how that feels, and I know what happens when that's taken away." Garrett didn't want to go back down that road yet again. "Like I said, I'll stay for a few more days as long as you won't get into any trouble."

53

The rain let up, lightening to a drizzle and then stopping altogether. The clouds began breaking up and the world seemed lighter, cleaner, and definitely clearer. Garrett stood next to Nigel. This was going to be hard on both of them, but it was his fault. He should have known the potential heartaches of what they were doing, even if Nigel hadn't.

"Maybe I should leave," Garrett said softly.

That was the last thing he wanted. This entire trip was supposed to be about him getting his head screwed on straight, and here he was, complicating things. It should have been simple: rent a boat, travel from island to island, spend time on the open sea, let some peace and quiet sink in and stress and turmoil slip away. But not a single plan for this trip seemed to have worked out the way he expected.

Nigel stared at him, blue eyes searching, even raking over him. "No. Stay. I need to accept what is happening." He walked around the fire and sat down on the blanket.

Garrett grabbed the bag of food, set it on the blanket as well, and pulled out what he'd brought. The sun disappeared once again, and soon it was raining, only this time not as hard. Still, neither of them would be going anywhere soon, unless they wanted to get soaked to the skin, so they sat together and ate slowly.

"Isn't your aunt going to worry about you out in this weather?"

"I don't think the rain will last much longer. I told her I would be camping again." Nigel smiled and swept his hand toward the entrance. "It is only water—it will not hurt me. I've camped in weather like this before. If it's windy or stormy, that's different, and then I have to stay in the house." He made a face. "My aunt is nice enough, and she's taken care of Jules and me for a long time, but sometimes...." He turned to look out at the ever-lightening sky and water.

"What?" Garrett set a paper plate on the blanket and pulled out some crackers.

Nigel took one and munched on it absently. "I used to sit here, looking out at the water, wondering what was out there." He pivoted around. "I've read hundreds, maybe thousands, of books, and in some way, all of them describe what the world looks like out there. I want to see it. I asked Aunt Phyllis about it, and she said the rest of the world is an ugly place, filled with selfish people who wouldn't understand me. She told me I was safe here and had everything I needed. Then she started to cry and asked if I was really that unhappy." He blinked and sighed.

"When was that?" Garrett asked.

"Last night. I have asked her about the outside world before, but last night, I asked when she thought Jules and I could leave the island. She said he and I were safer here."

Garrett took his hand. "Do you really want to leave?"

Nigel didn't answer or move for quite a while. "Maybe. I don't really know. I guess I'd like the choice, but I don't think I'm going to get one. Jules isn't going anywhere because he's still too young to leave, and I'm not going to leave him here alone." His shoulders slumped, and he pulled his knees up to his chest, hugging them for comfort. "Dammit. I used to think I could live here forever, and...." He curled his lip upward. "Look what you did."

"Yeah, I know...," Garrett said.

Nigel grinned. "I was joking. You didn't do anything other than stay here and be my friend." He scooted closer. "I always wondered what it would be like somewhere else, but it was never that important. I always had whatever I really wanted here." He unhooked his hands and touched Garrett's cheek. "But now I know that there's more... out there...."

The softness in Nigel's eyes touched Garrett's heart with a gentle caress that spread heat through the rest of him. Garrett longed to tell him just what was out there and the things he'd seen. For a second he wondered if he should tell Nigel that he agreed with his aunt, that the world was ugly. Garrett had seen just about everything awful a person could do to someone else. Then he paused, because he'd also experienced love and happiness, which he wouldn't trade anything for.

"What do you think?"

"About the outside world? I think when you're ready, you and Jules will need to find out for yourselves." It was a cop-out answer and he knew it. What could he say? Offer to take Nigel on his boat and just sail away? He curled his lips upward at the idea, actually smiling as he thought of spending days on the water with Nigel… and nights tucked up in bed together, the rocking of the boat covering up the way they played each other's bodies like fine violins. Garrett sighed. Maybe there was something to this lone, tropical-island living.

Nigel rolled his eyes, and Garrett got a view of just how young Nigel was. "I'm not stupid."

"I never said you were. But sometimes things happen in their own time." Garrett munched on a cracker and some cheese, watching Nigel closely, studying the line of his jaw and the light in his eyes, even as the sunlight from the clearing skies faded. Nigel added some wood to the fire, while Garrett dug into the bag and pulled out some Oreos. He handed one to Nigel, who looked at it as though it was something that had washed up on the beach. He smelled it and took a bite, then smiled and ate the rest. Of course, then Garrett had to show him how to untwist and eat them properly.

Garrett tried to imagine never having contact with the outside world. This island had to be some kind of ideal. There was no crime, no real danger, tropical breezes, the water and beach… what the heck more could anyone really want? Garrett lay back on the blanket, studying the rock ledge overhead. Its jagged, dark layers grew deeper as the sunlight faded, eventually reflecting light from the fire, bright daggers dancing off them.

"I came here because my life was a mess," he said quietly, placing his hands under his head. "I had really messed things up."

Nigel grabbed some more cookies, the bag rustling, before he lay down as well and rested his arm across Garrett's chest. "Really?"

"I almost shot someone." Garrett closed his eyes. "An unarmed man. I thought he had a gun—I could see it in his hand. I really could… or thought I did. But there was nothing there… not really. The captain thought I'd been working too hard, but I'd been working to forget."

"David?" Nigel asked, and Garrett wound his arm around Nigel's shoulders.

"Yeah. It was hard being alone and missing him all the time, so I worked to try to forget. And then I think I forgot how to not work and just took as many shifts as I could. Sometimes I worked until I couldn't stand up anymore." Garrett heaved a deep breath of tropical air and released it, trying to make himself feel clean again. "If I was alone and awake, I used to think about David, so I made sure I was too tired to do that."

"What about now?" Nigel gently patted Garrett's belly.

Garrett hesitated. "Now, things are different." He lay still, the gentleness in Nigel's caress soothing some broken part of him. It was hard to describe it, but Nigel's care and simple human kindness seemed to be stitching parts of his shattered being back together. "I don't feel as frantic or wound up, and there's nothing for me to hide behind here."

"I know. I spend a lot of time alone." Nigel turned onto his side. "So I know who I am and the person I want to be. There is no one to lie to here... including myself."

And maybe that was the most naive, yet profoundly enlightened, thought Garrett had ever heard.

"I can't see you hiding anything." Garrett opened his eyes to find Nigel's gaze drilling into him.

"You need honesty... like me." Nigel patted Garrett's chest as though he had all the answers to the universe's grand questions. "You must stop running and let yourself be caught." He leaned closer. "It's like when you hit your toe. It hurts, but you feel it, and you jump around and swear maybe. But then the pain fades and your toe turns ugly colors, and finally it heals and everything is all right."

Garrett chuckled as he tried to follow Nigel's point, his mind running at a slower speed than usual. "I think you're going to have to help me a little more than that."

"You are the toe," Nigel said seriously.

"Are you saying I'm stinky, like feet?"

Nigel laughed. "No. I'm saying you are the toe that got hurt, but you never jumped around or swore. You went to work. You never got all black-and-blue, and then you never healed." He cocked his eyebrows slightly. "You needed to let yourself feel the pain of loss so you could let it go. And Aunt Phyllis says that this is the best place to be when you're hurting. I think that's part of the reason why she brought me and Jules here. So we could heal." He had this clear glow in his eyes, like he was sure of the world and everything in it. Maybe he was. After all, Nigel's world and worries consisted of caring for his underwater collection of conches and protecting sea turtle eggs.

A spike of cold went through his chest. Garrett already had the feeling that things weren't quite as they appeared on this island. Now he wondered if he would be better off leaving things as they were. So what if Aunt Phyllis didn't look like Jules or Nigel? What if she wasn't their aunt? Nigel seemed happy and contented here. Who was he to intrude on that? This island was a break... a refuge from the worries and pain of the outside world, and by following Nigel to investigate, what if he was wrong about this whole situation and brought the outside world here in full force? What was going to harm Nigel more?

"Where did you go?" Nigel asked. "You were all scrunched and stiff."

Garrett chuckled. "Sorry. I guess maybe that was part of the black-and-blue-toe thing you were talking about." He tried to silence the conflict raging inside him. Whatever was happening here was none of his business. But the cop in him, once stirred, was itching to move forward. Part of him had to know, and yet... there were consequences to his actions, and one of them could very well be destroying Nigel's happiness. "I need to learn to let shit go."

Nigel snickered. "You better. It stinks." He held his nose, and Garrett laughed.

"It's just a saying. It means I need to stop worrying."

"Uh-huh." The rain had stopped a while ago, but water still dripped down the face of the overhanging rocks onto the sand. Nigel sat up to add some more wood to the fire. "When you go back, will the things that hurt... will they not still be there?"

Garrett wished he had an answer for that. "I suppose they will. But sometimes it isn't the problems that matter, but how we look at them." He hoped he'd be in a better headspace and then could move on.

Nigel leaned closer. "If you stayed here, then they would stay away and you could be happy."

It was a lovely thought, and at the moment, it was tempting to give the rest of the world a great big "fuck off." Hell, Garrett figured he could stay right here, under this outcropping, and be happy for a long time... as long as he had company.

"You know that isn't really possible. Your aunt. How would she feel? From what you've said, she doesn't take a liking to strangers."

Nigel sighed. "I know. I just don't want you to go."

"I know." Garrett wasn't looking forward to pulling up anchor and heading back out into the sea, but sooner or later, he would need to go, and Garrett suspected that sooner might be better. The longer he stayed, the more both of them were likely to get attached. "But—"

Nigel hummed and cut him off with a kiss. Leaving the words unsaid wasn't going to change anything... for either of them. But if it made Nigel feel better, then Garrett wouldn't challenge him.

Night fell around them and the fire grew dim. Garrett wasn't sure what he should do, but Nigel seemed to have ideas of his own, and once the flames of the fire lowered, Nigel added a few pieces of wood before slowly climbing onto Garret. Part of him wanted to resist, but Nigel's boundless energy and excitement swept that away. This was a very bad idea... at least logically, but his heart had already reached out to Nigel, and the heart wanted what it wanted... and he'd just started listening to it again.

GARRETT WOKE naked under the blanket, alone.

"I'm sorry. I didn't mean to wake you, but I have to get back," Nigel told him, kneeling nearby.

Garrett pushed back the covers, yawning as he stretched his back, looking for his clothes. They hadn't been very discriminating about where they tossed them in the darkness, and Garrett shook the sand out of them before slipping them on. "I'll help you put everything away."

Once he was dressed, he helped fold things up, and Nigel filled the duffel and placed it back in its spot outside the overhang. After climbing over the rockfall, Nigel kissed him goodbye and hurried off.

Garrett watched after him, his curiosity warring with discretion. "Oh, fuck it," he groaned, and took off into the woods after Nigel.

The path was fairly well worn and easy to follow for most of the way. Garrett kept quiet and went slowly, trying to remain hidden. The last thing he wanted was for Nigel to discover him. The forest was filled with scurries and rustles. Garrett concentrated and did his best not to get riled or spooked. On either side of him, the jungle thickened within a foot, so all he could see was a tunnel of green in front of him. Branches covered part of the path, and he moved them aside, stepping over limbs and fronds, until he spotted an off-white house, the paint weathered and worn in places. He could just make out the outlines of the building between breaks in the undergrowth. He didn't want to get too close. It seemed he had come up on the back of the house.

"Nigel, where were you?" said a teenager, probably Jules, as he raced up to Nigel at the front corner of the house. "I think the turtles are hatching. I can see movement in the sand. Do you want to come see?"

Garrett slowly moved closer, checking around him as he settled into the undergrowth, hoping to hell these plants didn't have prickers. Jules looked much as Garrett imagined him: a smaller version of Nigel, with the same blond hair and slender build. Jules was going to be handsome when he got older. Garrett's attention shifted to Nigel just as he turned the corner and disappeared from sight. Garrett didn't hear his answer, so he made his way around to the side of the house, staying under cover.

No one seemed to be around, and the surf pounded the beach nearby. That gave him cover for making noise, but it also made it hard for him to hear anything. Part of him wanted to see where Nigel and Garrett had gone, but they weren't really the objects of this visit. He went back the way he came and around to the other side of the house. A forty-foot cleared area near the building there made it hard for him to get too close without being seen.

Garrett wished he knew the layout of the building and where the others might be. It was still early in the day. He carefully sat under cover, with his back to Jules and Nigel's last location. Then he settled in to wait.

After about ten minutes, he wished he'd changed his pants before coming out here. Garrett swatted insects away from his legs and arms, doing his best to ignore them while continuing to watch, even as the heat of the day built. Sweat ran down his arms and forehead, and he realized he wasn't going to be able to stay here much longer without being eaten alive and roasted in the heat. Besides, sitting here wasn't getting him anywhere. There was no one about, and as far as he could see, no one moving inside.

He went around the back of the house, where there were few windows, keeping low, and skittered up against the building. He stayed under the windows, rising up just enough to hear if anyone was inside. He didn't hear any voices or movement, so Garrett continued around toward the front side of the house and crept under the windows. Humming reached his ears, soft and gentle. He was able to peer in just enough to see a woman in her forties, with jet-black hair and olive skin, sitting in a chair, rocking slowly as she did needlework. That must have been Aunt Phyllis, and Garrett had to agree with the lady in the village—she didn't look like Nigel or Jules in the least. Granted, that didn't mean she wasn't their aunt by marriage.

"Where have you been?" she asked, and Garrett slid lower against the house, staying out of sight under the window.

"Just checking on our charges," a man's voice said dryly. "Nigel has been camping out a lot lately. I wanted to make sure he's not sneaking over to the village."

"Has he been seen there?" Phyllis asked, and the man Garrett assumed was Fairfield didn't answer. "I know you have friends there."

Shit, Garrett had been careful when he visited and acted like he was leaving. He hoped the villagers had bought it and hadn't thought too much of his appearance.

"No. He hasn't. Someone else was—stopped for supplies and then left again, toward Martinique." He didn't seem concerned and there was no fear in his voice. "But—"

"What?" Something clinked on what sounded like glass.

"I followed Nigel yesterday, at least as far as the denser undergrowth. He said he was camping near Overlook Rock, but he went in the other direction." Suspicion rose in his voice, and Garrett felt his hackles rise. "I don't like it when he isn't truthful, and the other day, I thought I saw a sail approaching the island. If we have visitors and if they've talked with Nigel…."

"Come on. He knows nothing at all about anything. He's been here for over a decade. You're paranoid, and it's been getting worse for the last year. Relax and let them have the run of the island. It isn't as though they can get off or go anywhere. Let them be."

Garrett dared a quick look. A man, probably Fairfield, paced the room while Aunt Phyllis sat in her chair.

"I made a call, and others don't necessarily share your optimism, *Aunt* Phyllis," Fairfield snarled. Clearly the two of them didn't always get along. The derision in his tone left Garrett cold.

These people didn't have Jules and Nigel's best interests at heart. Someone else was pulling the strings.

"Those boys haven't done anything out of the ordinary, and you know it." The chair creaked, and Garrett pressed to the wall as he heard someone approach the window. "Just because you don't want to be here any longer is no reason to cause trouble for the rest of us." Her voice came from right above him. "Go and get yourself an Irish coffee or something and leave me and them alone." Now it was her turn to be derisive. "Or maybe I'll call and suggest that you need to be replaced. And you know what will happen then." She banged her hand on the windowsill.

"Bitch," Fairfield grumbled, and the door to the room opened and closed.

Phyllis stayed where she was, and Garrett's legs began to ache. He hoped to hell she moved soon or he would end up falling into a heap when his knees gave out, and then all hell would break loose.

"Aunt Phyllis!" Jules called as heavy footsteps raced into the room. "You have to come see! The turtles are hatching! They're emerging from the sand and swimming away. I wish I could keep one, but...." More footsteps followed, and then it was quiet again.

Garrett hurried back toward the foliage and under cover. He listened for some sort of uproar, but none followed. Garrett figured he'd pressed his luck already and it was time to go.

Some serious shit was going on, but he didn't know what it was. It seemed to him that Phyllis and Fairfield were here to watch the boys, maybe even hold them prisoner. Garrett had seen some fucked-up things, but this was weird on a whole new scale.

Part of him wanted to get the hell out of this looney bin. But he couldn't leave Nigel and Jules to the mercy of these people. He had to talk to Nigel and hope he could convince him. Maybe if he was persuasive, he could get the two of them onto his boat and away from here before the others found out. That would be a tall order, because Nigel was unlikely to believe him. It had been very clear from their conversations that he believed Phyllis—if that was her real name—to be his aunt, something Garrett now doubted was possible at all.

"That was so fun!" Jules said as he hurried along the path, his excitement ringing through the air. "They all just climbed out of the sand and into the waves. I thought there would be more to it than that, but nope."

"Did you check the nest?" Nigel asked.

"Yeah. There were a few who didn't make it. That's so sad." Jules stepped out of the trees, with Nigel behind him. "I suppose that's the survival of the fittest and all that. Only the strongest make it to the sea so they have a chance against all the predators and things." They stopped at the edge of the clearing near the house. "Now that I'm not going to be watching out for the eggs, what should I do?" He seemed a little lost.

"Why don't you check the beach for other nests? There are sure to be some. Or you could go fishing." Neither of Nigel's suggestions seemed to hold any interest, judging by Jules's disinterested body language. "There's plenty you can do."

"Nigel...." Jules shifted his weight from foot to foot, practically hopping.

"You could read some more. I'll set up a program for you for the next couple of weeks." Nigel looked sternly at Jules, who seemed about as interested as a kid going to the dentist. "I know you'd rather be out on the beach, but we have to learn about other things too." Nigel passed right in front of Garrett and rounded the corner of the house, his voice fading away.

Garrett figured now was as good a time as any, so he moved away from the house and headed toward the cove as quickly as he could. He reached the beach, grabbed the dinghy from where they'd stashed it, and headed out to the boat. Once back on board, he pulled up the dinghy and secured it to the deck before picking up his notebook and sitting in the shade. Garrett wrote down what he'd heard before the memories faded, as well as his impressions. He tried reconciling it with what Nigel had told him, but Nigel's story had holes the size of a Mack truck. He made up his mind that when he saw Nigel again, he would tell him what he'd heard.

Garrett checked the boat over as he walked the deck. There was no way in hell that Nigel would believe him or take him seriously. He had spent years with his so-called aunt, and she'd had plenty of time to earn his trust. Hell, Nigel probably loved her and wasn't going to turn his back on her. Garrett paused and sighed, wishing he had a way to keep an eye on Nigel.

His first partner, John Little—and if Garrett had called him Little John, he'd have ended up black-and-blue—always said, "We need proof. The truth doesn't mean shit without it." The words rang in Garrett's ears over and over again. "The truth doesn't mean shit without proof."

Great, and how was he supposed to get it? Sure, it was possible Aunt Phyllis and Fairfield might have gotten sloppy over the years and left something incriminating at the house, but that would be damned near impossible for him to get. Contrary to the movies, it was hard to break into a place one wasn't familiar with, and all it took was one shout and everything was over, including his life, most likely.

"Goddammit." He had to do something. His guts twisted first one way and then another as he watched the beach, waiting for Nigel to make an appearance, hoping he was okay. Garrett thought of going back to watch the house again—or if he were honest with himself, to watch Nigel. The thought of him being hurt sent fire running through Garrett's head, spreading out to sear his heart. He couldn't allow anyone to hurt Nigel.

"Okay. But what do I do?" he asked himself, hoping for an idea as he continued watching the beach. Garrett needed to devise some sort of plan. He was alone and had zero backup of any kind. Maybe he could take out both Fairfield and Phyllis, then pick up the pieces. But what if he was wrong? The possibility chilled him to the bone. One thing was clear: sitting here doing nothing wasn't helping anyone.

Garrett descended the stairs into the cabin and drank an entire bottle of water before opening some meal packets and eating as quickly as possible. He was going to need energy for the long haul.

Once he'd finished devouring everything he could eat, Garrett grabbed a couple bottles of water and tossed the dinghy into the waves, climbed in, and made for shore.

As he got out to haul the dinghy onto the sand, Nigel hurried up to him. Garrett jumped and then sighed with relief. "Glad you're here," he said, trying to sound normal, even as relief washed over him, followed by tension and a renewed worry. Just because Nigel was here now didn't mean he was truly safe. "I figured I'd spend the day here rather than on the boat." Finished securing the inflatable, he turned to Nigel, who was busy biting his lower lip. "What's wrong?"

"I don't know. Fairfield is acting bossy, and Aunt Phyllis is nervous." Nigel turned in the direction of the house. "She said it was best if we spent the day at the house. I didn't want you to worry, so I climbed out the window and hurried over here." He shrugged and then kissed Garrett quickly. "I have to go back, but I wanted to see you." Nigel kissed Garrett once again and then raced back into the foliage.

Garrett debated for about two seconds before following him. He had to know what was going on.

Nigel moved quickly, and Garrett hung back so he wouldn't be seen. He got halfway to the house before the hum of an engine caught his attention off to his left. He stopped and listened as the hum intensified. Garrett veered off in that direction just as it ceased, moving as fast as he dared along the path. This one was less used and more difficult to follow. He had to climb a small hill and over rocks and fallen trees before approaching the beach on the opposite side of the house. A speedboat—compact, sleek, and powerful—bobbed in the waves as two men pulled it up into the sand. A larger one was anchored offshore, and Garrett didn't need to get closer to see that it was sleek and expensive. Someone with money was behind whatever was going on.

Garrett settled out of sight as they secured the boat and reached inside. Holy shit! The men were huge and dressed in light clothes that could almost let them pass for tourists at a tropical resort. One had jet-black hair and was slightly overweight. The other was more fit, with brown hair. They both walked like their legs were too big for them.

"I don't get this," Brown Hair said as he leaned into the boat.

"Be quiet," Black Hair snapped. "We have our orders. Finish off the kids and take the other two back with us." He stopped to glare at his partner. "Just carry out our orders, and let's get out of here."

Garrett gasped as they both pulled guns out of the locker in the front of the boat and then headed up the beach at a slow jog toward the house. Ice shot through his veins. He stood still in shock for about two seconds, and then anger and determination took over. He'd be damned if he was going to let anything happen.

As soon as they were out of sight, Garrett sprinted across the sand to the boat. He checked the locker for another gun and came up empty. He swore and closed it before heading back into the undergrowth, racing toward the house as fast as he dared.

CHAPTER 6

A WIDE leaf smacked him in the face as he rushed through the dense growth, but Garrett barely felt it. He reached the path he'd veered off from and then continued on to the house.

"Garrett," Nigel said as he came closer, smiling.

"Where's Jules?" Garrett asked quickly, pulling Nigel to him and bringing him down to a crouch.

"Back at the house," Nigel answered. "What's going on?"

"There isn't time to explain." Garrett focused on getting the two of them safe. Then he could figure out what to do next. "It's for his safety."

Nigel bit his lower lip, clearly confused. He hesitated a second, then nodded, stood, and whistled like one of the birds that never seemed to shut up during the day. Nigel repeated the call, and sure as shit, Jules came down the path a minute later.

"Who is this?" Jules asked, wearing the same genuinely pleasant smile as Nigel.

"A friend of mine," Nigel answered before turning to Garrett.

"Take Jules to the overhang and stay there. Don't come out or let anyone know you're there until I call for you. Please. Just trust me and stay there. Don't make any noise or let anyone see you. Okay?" Garrett desperately willed Nigel to understand.

"Okay," Nigel agreed.

"Why?" Jules demanded.

"Because I think there are people here to hurt you... both of you."

Jules and Nigel both stood. "Then we have to help Aunt Phyllis." Nigel was already starting back toward the house.

"I'll help her," Garrett said. "Just go to the overhang and get under it where you can't be seen. Please." He was willing to beg Nigel if that was what it took.

Nigel looked toward the house, worrying his lip, and then nodded and took Jules by the hand, tugging him away from the house and down the path toward the beach.

As soon as they were out of sight, Garrett continued to the house. He had to eliminate the threat to Jules and Nigel. That was the only way to keep the two of them safe. The path to the beach was worn enough that if Garrett could follow it, then so could the men.

"Where are they?" a deep voice demanded, drifting on the air from the direction of the house. Then a skin-on-skin slap, followed by a short scream. "You fucking know." Another slap echoed.

Garrett stayed low and carefully made his way to the window.

"Just tell us and we'll take you with us. Otherwise...."

Garrett recognized the voice of the black-haired man. His menace hung in the air. Garrett managed a quick peek into the room. Both of them were with Phyllis. Garrett wished he knew where Fairfield was, even as he made his way around to the front.

"Just take it easy, both of you." So Fairfield was with them as well. At least Garrett knew where everyone was, but that didn't help him with a plan.

He peered around the corner, looking down the wide porch for something to use as a weapon. Near the door was an umbrella stand, but little else. Staying close to the house, he moved toward the front door, hoping to hell the floorboards didn't creak.

"They'll be back soon enough," Fairfield said. "In the meantime, one of you take her upstairs. The boss can deal with her when the time comes."

Garrett pressed his back to the outside wall as footsteps passed close to the door.

"You're hurting me," Phyllis complained.

"I'll do more than that if you don't shut up," Brown Hair said, and Phyllis squeaked again before heavy footsteps signaled their retreat.

Garrett could hear Fairfield and Black Hair talking in the other room as he slipped inside. The door entered into a living area with light furniture that had seen better days. Garrett grabbed a bronze horse from the table. He stood near the door to the room with the men and scratched on the wall just loudly enough to be heard.

"See what the fuck that is," Fairfield demanded.

Garrett held the sculpture over his head and brought it down on Black Hair's skull. The horse broke as the huge lug fell to the floor. Garrett wrenched the gun from his hand, shot Fairfield as he came through the door, and instantly turned toward the stairs, where Brown Hair leveled his gun at Garrett.

"Drop it," Brown Hair said.

Garrett held still, gun pointed. "Really?" He was prepared to take the bullet as long as he could drop this guy. "Now, Phyllis!" Garrett snapped, and the idiot turned at the ruse. Garrett pulled the trigger, sending Brown Hair spinning and collapsing onto the floor, wailing about his shoulder. Garret didn't really care. He snatched up Brown Hair's gun, brandishing both in case of trouble. At least now he had the firepower.

"Where the fuck did you come from?" Fairfield groaned.

He ignored him. "Phyllis, are you all right? Can you hear me?" Garrett called up the stairs.

"Yes. I'm fine," she called back, coming slowly down.

"Is there any rope?" he demanded.

She stayed on the landing, pressed to the wall. "Who are you?"

"The person who will shoot them and you if you don't do what I want." Garrett didn't trust her at all. "I took care of the men who hurt you, so just do what I need." He waved the gun, and she came down and hurried toward the back of the house. She returned with some lengths of clothesline. Garrett trussed up Fairfield, listening to him whine but not giving a damn about his leg. Garrett did the same with the brown-haired thug, making sure the ropes were tight.

"I'm bleeding," Brown Hair groaned, trying to fight.

Garrett leaned down. "Like I care. If you're lucky, I might call someone to help you. Otherwise you'll stay right where you are. I'm a police officer, and I know how to take care of guys." He stared into his brown eyes, which filled with fear by the second. "Now, don't move, or I'll tighten the ropes." Once satisfied, he tied up the last man and stepped back from his handiwork. All three were trussed up like hogs, and it would take some time for any of them to get out.

"Phyllis." He turned to the so-called aunt.

"Where are the boys?" she asked, nearly frantic.

He shook his head, went to the doorway, and motioned with the gun.

Phyllis slowly stepped forward, watching him diligently, her eyes following him as though she expected to be shot at any second. "What do you want?"

He motioned for her to step away from the house, grabbed one of the porch chairs with his free hand, and placed it in the yard. "Sit down."

She complied, her eyes darting around.

"I need some answers, and that's the only reason you're still alive." He stepped closer, keeping the gun on her.

"Where are Jules and Nigel?" she asked again. "That's all I care about."

Garrett scoffed. "Really? That's interesting. Is that why you held them prisoner here for eleven years?" He met her gaze, and she had the decency to look ashamed.

"I did it to keep them safe." She said it with such ease, and Garrett wondered how she could lie so easily.

"I heard your conversations with Mr. Belvedere in there, and I know you were working for someone. So don't try to hand me a line of shit. Nigel and Jules are safe, and they'll remain that way if I have to kill those guys in there and you to do it." He had never killed anyone in cold blood, and he didn't think he had it in him, not if push came to shove, but she didn't know that. "First, you're not their aunt. Let's get that straight."

"No. After their parents died, I was hired to bring them here and watch over them." She looked about ready to cry, but he wasn't having any crocodile tears. "Look, I'll tell you… and them… everything you want to know. But I just have to know they're all right. I've cared for them for all this time, and I don't want to see them hurt." For some reason he believed her—maybe it was the way she held his gaze, her eyes pleading—but he remained cautious.

"Why should I accept anything you say as the truth?" Garrett asked.

"Because they're still in danger. When those men or Fairfield don't report in, our employer is going to know something is wrong and he's going to send more people to investigate." She became even more nervous, and Garrett wondered who she was more afraid of, him or her employer.

"First things first—are there more than just the two?"

Phyllis shook her head.

"There's communication equipment?" Garrett asked, and she nodded. "Take me to it." He motioned her to her feet. "And do you have anything to make our friends sleepy?"

She nodded and led him inside. Garrett kept his gun on her, and they walked through the room past the men to the back of the house. She pulled open a bank of cabinets to reveal a small room with a satellite communication system. There was also a medicine cabinet, which she opened and pulled out a syringe. "Fairfield kept this on hand in case the boys became trouble. It will put them to sleep for six hours or so."

The irony wasn't lost on Garrett.

"Perfect. Set it on the counter and step away." He took the syringe and administered a dose to each of the three men. Once they were out, he could relax a little before returning to the satellite equipment. He picked up the receiver, and she touched his hand.

"This line is monitored. As soon as you make a call, they will know who it was to."

Garrett placed the handset back in the cradle and stepped back, then fired two bullets into the equipment, shorting it out. "Get some food and water for the boys, now. Pack lightly, but take what you can carry. We're leaving this place." He let her load a bag with provisions, and then they went upstairs, where she packed some clothes for Jules and Nigel, as well as herself. When they were finished, they descended the stairs and left the house, the three men sleeping on the floor.

"Should we leave them without any hope of rescue?" Phyllis asked.

"Once we're away, I'll report this, but until then, they can stay right there." Garrett hadn't wounded any of them too badly, and they'd wake up in a few hours. They could take their chances after that. "We're leaving." He loaded Phyllis down with the bags and directed her around the back of the house.

"You don't need that gun. I'm not going to attack you or try to run away," she said as she hesitated at the entrance to the trail. "I care about those boys. You have to believe me."

He placed the gun in his belt on the opposite side of the other one and pointed to the trail. "You'll regret breaking your word." He flashed her a searing gaze until she squirmed and nodded. "Go on ahead. I'll be right behind you." Garrett waited until she stepped into the jungle before following.

THEY WALKED out onto the beach a while later. Phyllis turned to where his boat rocked in the waves. "How long have you been here?"

"About a week." Had it only been that long? It seemed like longer, but then his thoughts had been consumed by one particular person.

"And you know Nigel and Jules?" Her upper lip turned and her eyes hardened. "What did you do to them?"

"I only met Nigel, and they're fine and safe. Unlike you, I'd never hurt either of them or hold them hostage. Nigel is an incredible person, and he deserves better than the life you allowed him to have."

Phyllis rolled her eyes. "You don't understand at all." She put her hands on her hips.

"Maybe I don't, but then neither do Nigel and Jules. They've been kept here, away from the rest of the world, with no thought to how they felt about it." Garrett stepped closer. "You took away their choices, their freedoms, and their childhood. They never had friends to play with or got to see anything beyond this island."

"This is a good place," she countered.

"Maybe. But how good is it when men show up to kill them?" He wasn't going to let this go, and as Phyllis's shoulders slumped, he knew he'd finally gotten through to her in some way.

"I'll tell them everything." She sighed. "Yes, I helped keep them here, I admit that. But sending men to kill them is more than I ever agreed to." Her right hand shook, and Garrett allowed for the possibility that she was telling the truth. "I don't want those boys hurt. How many times can I say that? Why do you think Fairfield wanted me out of the way as well?" She turned toward the water, staring outward. "I love those boys. I'm probably the only one who does."

She has one hell of a way of showing it. Garrett shook his head, wondering if all the time here on the island had warped her brain. To him that wasn't love. Allowing the ones you cared for to make their own decisions and live their lives openly and to have choices—that was love. Not hiding them away.

"You stay here, and I'll go see if Nigel and Jules want to talk to you." He placed his hand on a gun to emphasize his point, walked over to the rockfall, and climbed to the top. "Nigel, it's me."

A shadow moved under the ledge, and then Nigel peered out from under the overhang. "What's happened?"

Garrett had to remind himself that they knew nothing about any of this. "It's safe now. And I have Phyllis with me. Why don't both of you come with me?" He waited for them to come out and join him. As soon as they climbed over the rockfall and got onto the beach, they ran to Phyllis and hugged her tightly, nearly knocking her over. Garrett joined them and met Phyllis's gaze.

"What are these bags for?" Jules asked, pointing to the gray duffels at Phyllis's feet.

"I have some things to tell you." She motioned for them to sit. "You both deserve to know the truth. I probably should have told you a long time ago and figured out how to get you off this island."

Garrett stayed close to her in case she made any move to hurt Nigel or Jules, but she seemed gentle with both of them.

"What is it?" Jules shifted to sit right next to her.

Phyllis put an arm around Jules and turned to Nigel. "Do you remember when your parents died?"

Nigel and Jules nodded.

"You were so young and small, and I always wanted a boy just like you," she said to Jules and then swallowed and looked at Garrett.

"You need to tell them everything," he said, kneeling down. Garrett wished he knew what she was going to say so he could prepare them. "They deserve to know."

"Know what?" Nigel asked, taking Jules's hand as tension built around them.

Garrett gave Phyllis a "you tell them or I will" look.

"That day I met you at your house, there was another man," she said with a nod. "His name was Hilliard and he is your uncle, your father's brother. I also told you that I was your aunt, but that was a lie. Is a lie. I'm not your aunt."

Nigel and Jules tensed, and Jules pulled away.

"I was hired by your uncle to pose as your aunt, his sister." She raised her gaze again.

"The truth, Phyllis," Garrett said, and then turned to Nigel and Jules. "It's been denied to both of you for a long time, and you deserve to know what's really been going on so you can decide what you want to do."

"I know." She hung her head as Nigel slid away from her and moved next to Garrett. Garrett put an arm around Nigel's waist as Jules sat holding Nigel's other hand.

"Just tell us," Nigel said firmly.

"Your uncle hired me and Fairfield to bring you here and watch over you. This island is his and so is the house. I was supposed to pose as your aunt and Fairfield as our caretaker. But his real job was to make sure neither of you found out what was really happening."

"Who is this uncle?" Garrett asked.

Phyllis held her breath for a second and then blew it out. "Hilliard Huntington Montague."

Garrett's legs nearly fell out from under him. "As in HM Consulting, HM Finance, HM Hotels, Hilliard Montague?"

"Yes," Phyllis answered, and both boys looked to him for answers.

"He's one of the richest men in the country," Garrett supplied, and Phyllis nodded slowly.

"I think you all need to listen closely." She cleared her throat, and Garrett shifted away slightly with the boys, leaving Phyllis alone, with the bags separating them. That seemed to work for Nigel and Jules, and Garrett wasn't going to change that. He held Nigel as tightly as he could, just to let him know he wasn't alone as the foundations of his entire world and everything he thought he knew crumbled from under him.

"Just tell us!" Jules snapped, and Nigel tugged him closer. It felt as though they were drawing strength from him, and Garrett let them. He'd already determined that he'd be there for both of them.

"I don't know the details—your uncle didn't tell them to me—but I believe from what I've been able to piece together over the years that your father was a brilliant man. He took what was a small family fortune and built it into a huge number of successful businesses. He was a visionary. When he died, he left everything to the two of you. Your uncle was to act as trustee until Nigel turned twenty-one. Then he was to come into his inheritance."

Garrett swore under his breath. "He wanted to remain in control of everything. So Hilliard set all of you up here?"

"Yes. No kids, no interference with what he wanted to do. He had control of billions, and with them out of the way, things would stay that way. It was my job to make sure Jules and Nigel stayed on the island and were oblivious to the outside world. It seemed to be working." She sniffed. "We gave both of you the run of the island, and you seemed happy. That was all I wanted."

"You were hired and paid all these years?" Nigel asked, hurt ringing in his voice.

"Yes. But you have to believe me. I care for both of you."

Jules scoffed the way only a teenager could. "You're full of crap."

"No. I do care. That's why I'm here." Phyllis turned to look out to sea. "Fairfield was getting nervous because you'd been spending a lot of time away from the house, and then there were rumors in the village that you had met someone." She sighed, then turned to Garrett. "He was in the village, and someone mentioned that they'd met you. Fairfield has friends there who report back to him on occasion. Anyway, he started getting edgy and worried that you had talked to Nigel and that you might have figured out what was going on. He called Hilliard…."

Garrett turned to Jules and Nigel. "Your uncle sent two men to kill you. Neither of you had been seen in years, so he probably thought he could do whatever he wanted. It wasn't likely there would be any questions, and I suspect neither of you would have been found."

"Is that why you sent us here?" Nigel asked, as shook up as Garrett had seen anyone in all his years in law enforcement.

"Yes. I had to know that both of you were safe no matter what."

"Where are they?" Jules asked. That kid had one hell of a backbone.

"He shot them and Fairfield. They're tied up in the house," Phyllis said. "He went to great lengths to protect both of you. And he even saved me."

Garrett was still deciding if that was a good decision or not.

"He also destroyed the satellite phone that Fairfield and I used to communicate with your uncle."

"What do we do now?" Nigel asked as both he and Jules turned to Garrett.

"That's up to you. The men have a boat. It's on the other side of the island. I don't want them to be able to use it to get away if they get loose."

Nigel stood. "I'll take the launch they used and remove the spark plugs so they can't go anywhere. I can get over there fast, since I know the island better than you do."

"Do you know how to do that?" Garrett asked.

Nigel rolled his eyes. "I read a lot of books. I know how engines work."

"Okay. While you're gone, we'll transfer what Phyllis grabbed for both of you and the supplies to the sailboat."

"Then we leave?" Jules asked, glancing between him and Nigel, who thought a few minutes.

"Yes. We leave the island. Help Garrett get our things on board, and I'll be back as soon as I can." Nigel turned and hurried away, waving before disappearing down the path.

Garrett watched him go, unable to take his gaze away until Nigel disappeared. Then he picked up the two bags and carted them over to the rubber dinghy. "Let's get this on board and stowed. Somewhere above the rock ledge, Nigel keeps a bag of camping gear. Do you know where it is?" he asked Jules, not so much because he needed it, but because he wanted to give him something to do.

"Yes. He took me camping here. I know where he keeps it." Jules raced away and over the rockfall.

Garrett turned back to Phyllis, whose shoulders slumped and eyes drooped a little.

"They don't understand what I did for them," she whispered.

"I think it's what you did *to them* that they are going to have a hard time forgiving." Garrett set the food and other supplies on the dinghy and pushed it into the small waves. "Come on. You need to help me get this to the boat." He put her to work with a paddle.

Once at the sailboat, Garrett loaded everything they'd brought and put it away while Phyllis sat on the deck. He didn't trust her and wasn't likely to in the future. Garrett didn't want to leave her alone, but it was quickly becoming apparent that he had to. The dinghy was only going to hold three people at most. Thankfully Nigel and Jules weren't big guys.

He did lock the wheel in place and take the trolling engine keys with him as well before heading back to the beach. Garrett was still nervous about leaving her on the boat alone, but it was unavoidable.

Jules met him at the beach with the camping gear, and they loaded the dinghy.

"I'm sorry you have to go through all this," Garrett said, and Jules shrugged. What the hell did he say to someone when their world had been completely flipped on its ear? He decided to try a different topic. "Nigel told me about the turtles. I wish I could have seen them."

Jules lifted his gaze, some of the misery in his eyes fading. "It was so amazing. They hatched and all hurried to the water. I stood out of the way and watched them go. I wanted to keep one, but that wouldn't be fair to them. They all need to grow and have a chance to get big in the sea and maybe come back." He sat down, staring at the sand. "I hoped that maybe one of them would come back and lay eggs here and I could find another nest...."

"You can probably come back here again when you're older if you like." Garrett wanted to provide some sort of comfort, but he didn't know Jules, and the teenager wrapped his arms around himself, turning to stare at where the beach ended and dense greenery began. Garrett knew he was waiting for Nigel. He sat on the sand next to him. "I know you don't know me, but I'm a police officer. I was down here on vacation and ended up in the cove as shelter from the recent storm."

"I remember that," Jules said.

"I met your brother the following morning, and he showed me his collection and we talked... a lot." Garrett smiled. "I'm going to need you to trust me. I won't hurt you, no matter what."

"Do you like my brother? I saw the way you looked at him. It's the same way the boys look at the girls in the village." Jules didn't seem to mind or be concerned, and his tone was the same as most teenagers would use to ask about their favorite flavor of ice cream.

"Yes, I do. And I want to make sure you're both safe, and the best way to do that is to get out of here." Garrett sighed. "I shot three men and tied them up at the house. Phyllis told me that if they don't call in—and they can't now—your uncle will send more men to find out what's going on. And when he does, I want all of us to be long gone."

Jules nodded. "Where are we going?"

"First to Martinique to get more supplies." Garrett swore under his breath. Jules and Nigel were going to need travel documents and proof of citizenship if he was going to be able to get them into the US. He had been so intent on getting them all to safety that he hadn't asked about things like that. "Once we get somewhere safe, I will call my superiors in the police department, and they will help get us what we need to get back into the country." He certainly hoped so. "Is that okay?"

Jules turned to him like he was speaking gibberish. "You're asking me?"

"Yes. That's my plan. I want to help, but I'm not going to force you." Garrett really hoped Jules decided to go with him, but he wasn't going to kidnap him the way his uncle had. "I'm taking Phyllis as well. She is going to have to help by telling her side of the story."

"Will she be in trouble?" Jules asked.

"She might. But that isn't up to me. If she helps us, that will help her." It was the best he could do. Right then, he had to get both Jules and Nigel to safety.

"This is my home. But—" Jules paused as Nigel stepped out from the trees.

"How did it go?" Garrett asked him.

"They aren't going anywhere, and I hid their dinghy. If they get loose, they'll have to swim, and that's going to hurt." Nigel tossed Garrett the spark plugs. "Dead in the water." Then he went over and hugged Jules. "Are you okay?"

Jules nodded. "Garrett was asking me what I wanted to do, and I don't know."

Nigel sighed. "Garrett asks a lot of questions, but it's because he wants to know, not because he's trying to find out where you are or everything you've been doing like Fairfield always did." He glanced out at the sailboat. "We both used to think that we were cared about and…." He sighed, holding his brother tighter. "Garrett is a good man, I believe that."

"We'll go, then." Jules pulled back. "He said we need to get away, so let's do that." He hefted the last of the bags and put them in the dinghy. It was a little heavy, but they paddled out to the sailboat and got on board and got everything stowed. Then Garrett started the engine and, with Nigel's help, pulled up the anchor, and they glided out of the cove and into open water.

CHAPTER 7

GARRETT LOVED being on the water with the sails up, just the sound of the wind rushing past. There was nothing like sailing—he was one with the air and sea. Cruising under motor power always seemed choppy, but sailboats cut through the waves and seemed closer to the water, a part of it, so they gave a smoother ride.

Nigel and Jules sat on the deck, sharing the shade. They had been under sail for a few hours, and Garrett's GPS indicated they had another hour's journey before reaching Martinique. Then Garret could find a place to berth and figure out where to go from there.

"Where are we going to sleep?" Jules asked after a while. It was the first question Garrett had gotten from either of them since they set sail. They'd talked between them, but not to him or Phyllis. Probably with good reason.

"We have a few hours of light, so we'll find a sheltered cove or a town with a marina." He was hoping to stay off the grid as much as possible, putting as much distance as he could between them and danger. "How long before someone becomes suspicious?" Garrett asked Phyllis.

"They are already. It will take time to get someone to the island, but I'm willing to bet Hilliard has already sent someone down. Fairfield would have called in to report on anything that happened, and when Hilliard doesn't hear anything…."

"And he's going to expect us to make for Martinique simply because it's close. As long as the weather holds, we're going to keep going. Try for Dominica and see if we have any luck." The more Garrett thought about it, the more he realized he should steer clear of Martinique if at all possible. With Hilliard's land belonging to Martinique, it was likely he had connections there. The skies were clear and nearly cloudless, so that boded well for them. Garrett turned to Jules. "As for sleeping, I thought you and Nigel could take the main bed. The table folds down for Phyllis, and I can try to find some other space to sleep." He intended to stay on deck and keep a watch. If someone was after them, Garrett had no intention of being taken by surprise. "Is that okay?"

Jules nodded and pulled his legs up to his chest, hugging them with his arms. Nigel and Jules had lost everything they thought they knew... their home, even parts of themselves. The history they'd thought they had, had turned out to be a lie. How did anyone come back from that?

"There's the island." Jules pointed.

"Yup. I think we're going to stay on the west side of it to help remain in calmer waters. If we have to, we can go to a harbor, but for now, I think we'll just pass her by. I'm afraid your uncle will have contacts and influence there." Garrett steered offshore, and they continued on. The wind was steady, and as darkness fell, he turned on the running lights and kept going. He knew he was taking a chance by passing Martinique, but it was a measured risk. "Nigel," he called softly, "can you take the wheel?"

Nigel came over and sat next to him.

"Just hold the wheel. See that light right over there? Just keep it to starboard and stay as straight on as you can. I'm going to get the beds made up and everyone else settled." He let Nigel take hold and went below.

It took him half an hour to get all the beds made up. "This is for you and Nigel. Just pull the curtain if you want some privacy. Phyllis, this is for you. It's a little cramped...."

"I'll be fine. Thank you." She lay down, and Jules followed him topside.

Garrett took the wheel again and made a slight course correction, following the GPS. "Those lights are on Martinique, and we're going to pass the north end of the island soon." He sat and held the wheel, the sails full of wind, the seas rolling slightly. It was a perfect night. "I'd suggest that both of you get some sleep. There is going to be a lot to do tomorrow." He said good night to Jules, who went back below, and then kissed Nigel good night.

"Thank you for everything," Nigel whispered, then joined Jules below.

That left Garrett alone with the sea and wind, and he steered the sailboat, leaving the island behind them. No other darkness is like the dark in the middle of the sea with a new moon. Just the stars to point the way and the GPS screen for company. Granted, the distance to the island wasn't that great.

He sat quietly for a long while, enjoying the night, with no sounds coming from below. He guessed everyone was asleep, and he wished he and Nigel were curled up together on that bed.

"Garrett." The cabin door opened and Nigel came around to sit next to him.

"Couldn't sleep?"

He shook his head. "Jules is a kicker. He always moves a lot at night, so I thought I'd give him a chance to settle down." Nigel leaned against him, and Garrett put an arm around his shoulders as they slid through the night.

Eventually Nigel fell asleep. Garrett held him as lights shone on the horizon. Initially he wasn't sure he was seeing correctly, but more joined the first, signaling Dominica approaching on the horizon. He consulted the manual and radioed ahead. The harbor in Roseau answered, and he followed the directions to a berth. Gently he settled Nigel on the bench seat, tied up the boat, and went to deal with the business at hand.

He returned from the harbormaster's office an hour later with his berth paid for. Nigel was still asleep on the bench, curled up, using a chair cushion as a pillow. Garrett gently encircled him with his arms, carefully helping him below, and placed Nigel in the bed after scooting his bed-hog brother over.

"I'm okay," Nigel mumbled.

"Just sleep. We're safe and docked." Nigel rolled over, and Garrett watched him for a few minutes. He sighed before returning to the deck and stretching out in what he hoped would be the shade, closing his eyes. They were safe for now, and once the sun came up and he was rested and able to think straight, he could figure out a plan.

GARRETT WOKE some time later, the sun shining around him. At first he wondered what was wrong, until he turned over. Nigel lay next to him on the pad he'd thrown on the decking, a hand under his head, eyes closed, angelic expression on his face. Garrett didn't want to move in case he woke Nigel, but motion from the deck did that anyway.

"You should have stayed in bed."

"Jules is a hazard," Nigel said as he sat up, stretching. "And I wanted to be with you." He closed the distance between them. "I want to be with you like we were in the cave."

Garrett swallowed hard. His mind constantly returned to that night and how close they'd been. There was no way he could possibly forget it. "Me too." He sat up and hugged Nigel tightly. He couldn't do more than that right now, but part of him needed—craved—the closeness and intimacy.

"Nigel," Jules called, and Nigel sighed, getting up and going below.

Garrett watched him leave and tried to make his mind work. They needed food, and then Garrett had to make some phone calls. "We're in Dominica," he called down. "Get dressed, and we'll go find some food to start the day. Pack water to be safe." He waited until the others were done and sitting on deck before going below and digging out his cell phone. After changing and getting cleaned up, he led them all off the boat and down the dock to enter the town.

There were a few places open at one of the restaurants, and the four of them took seats. The food was basic Caribbean and looked good. After Garrett made sure they would take US dollars, they placed their orders. While the others stayed behind, Garrett stepped away from the table and made a call to the station at home.

"I need to speak with Captain Rodriguez," he told the operator. "At home if necessary." He waited a few minutes.

"Wreckley, what do you need? You're on vacation. Did you get into trouble or something?" he asked with a hint of concern in his voice.

"In a manner of speaking." Garrett sighed. "Does the name Hilliard Huntington Montague mean anything to you?"

The captain paused. "The billionaire? I've heard of him."

"Okay. It's a long story, but I need your help." He filled the captain in on what he'd discovered on the island, talking faster and faster as he went on.

"Holy shit. You go on vacation and step into a huge mess." The captain chuckled. "Bring me up to speed."

"I have Nigel and Jules, along with Phyllis. We're in Dominica now, and I'm willing to bet that Hilliard is trying to find us. We're going to stay here a few days and then continue heading north."

"What do you need?" the captain asked quickly.

"I'm going to check to see if the boys have any papers. I'm willing to bet they don't. But we're going to have to be careful, because Hilliard is going to be on the lookout for anyone showing interest in these boys. They're a huge threat to him, so much so that he was willing to have them killed." Garrett looked back at Nigel and smiled to hide the seriousness of the conversation.

"Let me make a few calls to some contacts I trust. You stay safe and keep under the radar." The captain sighed. "You know, I really should tell you to get your ass back here and not get messed up in shit like this...."

"Yeah?" Garrett groaned.

"But I'd probably do the exact same thing you are. So, stay safe and keep the boys safe too. I'll get back to you at this number." After Garrett agreed, the captain hung up.

Garrett returned to the table and dug into his breakfast with gusto.

"Is help coming?" Jules asked.

Garrett wasn't going to go into any details with Phyllis within hearing. He didn't trust her not to get word back. And until he did trust her, he was going to hold his cards close to the vest. "It will be."

He shared a smile with Nigel and shoveled his food into his mouth, feeling like he hadn't eaten in days.

Once they were done, he paid the bill, and they walked through the downtown. The boys looked in every shop window, and Garrett got both Jules and Nigel some fresh clothes, hats, and shoes, which seemed to make them happy. Then, after getting some more to drink, they walked back.

As they approached the dock, he saw two men standing right next to the sailboat.

"Do you know them?" Garrett asked Phyllis, who shook her head. "Fine. You stay with me. Nigel, take Jules back to town." He handed him some money and leaned close. "Go where we bought the shoes and stay in the back of the store. I'll come get you."

Nigel nodded, and the two of them took off.

Garrett, wishing he'd thought to take the guns with him, stepped onto the dock. "Can I help you gentlemen?" he asked.

The men turned to him, grim expressions firmly ensconced. "You came in last night?" the larger man asked.

"Yes." Garrett wasn't going to volunteer information until he knew what they wanted and who was behind their visit. Phyllis stayed behind him, out of their view.

"Why?" the man demanded.

Garrett slowly reached into his back pocket and withdrew his wallet. "I'm a police officer in Baltimore, Maryland." He showed them the identification, and the men's shoulders seemed to relax. "What are you worried about?"

"We have people bringing drugs in," he explained. "Especially at night."

"I see. No drugs. I'm on vacation and have been at sea for a while." He didn't want them to search the boat in case they came across Jules's and Nigel's things. That would bring additional questions he didn't want to answer. "And I've never been to Dominica and wanted to see it. A friend told me how beautiful it was, and I just had to make a stop."

The man smiled and nodded as though it were obvious that his island was the best in the entire world. "Who is she?"

Garrett winked. "She's a friend. I needed someone to cook and help take care of me."

The men glanced at each other, sharing a knowing look, and then grinned and stepped back. "We'll leave you to your vacation. Will you be staying long?"

"A few days. I want to look around and relax for a while. Maybe take in some of the beaches." Garrett smiled, and they nodded and walked back down toward the entrance.

"Those men thought I was some sort of floozy," Phyllis hissed as soon as they were out of sight.

"They thought you and I were closer than we are, yes. That's exactly what I wanted them to think. They didn't ask more questions, and the fewer people who know about Jules and Nigel, the better. It doesn't matter what they think as long as the boys are safe."

"What do we do now? Are they going to be watching us?"

"Probably not. But you stay here and make a show of doing chores around the boat. It doesn't matter what, just look busy and productive. Give them nothing to watch if they are. I'm going to get Nigel and Jules. They have to be worried. Can I trust you to do that?"

"Yes. I want them to be safe too." She climbed onto the boat and went below.

As Garret headed back down the dock, he turned and saw Phyllis hang bedding over the lowered sail to air it out, seeming ready to give the boat the cleaning of its life.

He turned and leisurely made his way back toward the business district. He didn't want to seem like he was going anywhere special, so he stopped in a few shops before ducking into the general merchandise market, where he found Nigel and Jules in the back, wound as tight as drums, practically vibrating with worry. "It's okay. They weren't looking for you." He watched the door for a pair of familiar faces, and seeing none, they left the store.

Heading down the way, they found a sweet shop. Jules and Nigel entered the small shop, wide-eyed, looking from wall to wall.

By US standards, the store was relatively subdued, but to two guys who had probably never seen a place like it in their lives, it must have seemed magical.

"You can get whatever you like."

"Really?" Jules asked.

"Anything you want." Garrett gathered some wrapped hard candy and chocolates on the counter and watched as the boys scoured the store before making their choices. He paid for it all, and they walked back through the town toward the waterfront. "Is it good?"

Jules nodded, popping a second butterscotch into his mouth with a grin. He practically skipped with excitement.

"It was like Willy Wonka," Nigel said, bumping Garrett's shoulder as they shared a smile.

"Maybe a little." Garrett's heart skipped a beat. He loved that he had been able to make Nigel happy. Hell, it made his heart lighter and his spirit more joyful, something he hadn't thought was possible for him to feel once again.

"Are you going to have some?" Jules asked, holding out the bag of loot.

Garrett picked out an orange hard candy, popped it into his mouth, and handed the bag back. "Don't eat too much all at once. The sugar will make you jittery." Jules had enough energy already. Hopped up on a load of sugar, he was going to go out of his skin.

"How long are we going to stay?" Nigel asked.

"A few days, I think. I have a friend who is working to help us, and I need to give him time. But we also need to be ready to go in a hurry if we have to."

When they approached the dock, the boat looked like a laundry line run amok. Phyllis stood on the deck, hands on her hips, surveying her handiwork.

"What's this?" Jules asked as he jumped aboard. "A laundry scow?" The kid had a smart mouth.

"Be nice," Nigel scolded lightly as Phyllis finished folding the bedding.

"I thought it could all use a good airing in the sun," she explained.

Garrett climbed onto the boat, his phone ringing as soon as he stepped on deck. He went to the back and sat where he could watch the harbor to answer it.

"Captain," he said softly.

"You were right. I called a few buddies in New York, and it seems that lawyers and authorities there have been trying to locate Nigel and Jules for years now. Their uncle has roadblocked them at every step, and since he technically had custody, there was nothing they could do." He cleared his throat. "One of my contacts, an old buddy from college, actually told me that they feared they were already dead. Of course, they couldn't prove it."

"Nope. He simply kept them out of the way and off the map for over a decade."

"You're going to need proof of everything. This guy isn't going to take any of this lying down," the captain said, and Garrett's gaze wandered to where Nigel stood outside the cabin. As he handed bedding below, Nigel turned to smile at him. Instantly Garrett shifted his legs so he wasn't obvious, and returned the smile. "Are you listening to me?"

Dammit, the captain had been talking and he'd taken a trip to happy land. "Sorry."

"What's going on there?" he pressed.

"Nothing. I was just watching to remain vigilant." Yeah, he lied, but he wasn't going to tell his boss that taking his gaze away from Nigel was damned near impossible. "I'll be careful here, and I have proof. The boys know the story now, and one of them is an adult. He's perfectly capable of managing his own life and affairs. And their caretaker will be a good witness."

"Too good?" Captain Rodriguez said. "Look, Montague is going to want to get rid of her just as badly as he will want to eliminate those boys. I spoke with one of their father's lawyers. Get them to a US port—any port—and he can meet you there and will have papers to help the boys enter the country. And I suggest you get them there fast."

Garrett sighed. He'd been hoping they could rest a little, but it wasn't in the cards. "Okay. We're docked at the moment. I need to give the boys a chance to stretch their legs." He'd paid for two days, so he was covered, and no one was going to complain if he left early. "I'll call you before we leave to check in."

"Do that. I'll message with any more information. Stay safe."

Garrett ended the call and shoved his phone in his pocket.

Nigel sat down next to him and leaned against his side. "Your face is all scrunchy. How bad is it?" he asked, and Garrett glanced at Jules, who was brushing off the deck cushions. He didn't seem to mind Nigel and him being affectionate. "I told Jules about us." Nigel seemed pleased.

Garrett swallowed. "You did?"

"Yeah. He said it was okay. He liked one of the girls from the village, but that was before Fairfield stopped us from going there." Nigel closed his eyes. "You didn't answer my question."

"We're going to need to leave soon," Garrett explained. He didn't want to go into all the details, but then decided that Nigel deserved to know. "My captain, the man I work for back home, looked into things." He turned to meet Nigel's gaze. "Your uncle isn't going to take this lightly. He's going to want to get you and Jules and… your uncle is going to kill Phyllis if he can get to her. She's a powerful witness to everything he's done, so he isn't going to let her live."

"Oh," Nigel whispered, pressing his face to Garrett's shirt. Garrett held him and let him cry. All the change and everything that had happened must have caught up with him. Tears threatened for him as well, but he kept strong and comforted Nigel.

"I know," Garrett said softly, and Nigel pulled away, his cheeks wet. "I know what it feels like to have your entire world ripped away from you. It sucks, and you have every right to be upset." He gently ran his thumb over Nigel's cheek. "I promise you I'll do anything I have to in order to keep you safe."

Nigel nodded. "But what do I do? I have no home, nothing. It's all gone." He blinked, and Garrett could tell he was trying so hard to keep it together, which only touched Garrett's heart even further.

"You'll make your own home. Once this is over, I'll help you and Jules make a home of your own. Maybe you can go back to the island, if that's what you want. We'll figure it out. But you don't have to worry about not having a home." Hell, they would always have one with Garrett if that was what they wanted. Garrett drew Nigel closer once again, just holding him, comforting, even daring to wonder what it would be like to be able to hold him for the rest of his life.

After a while, he noticed Phyllis and Jules were no longer on deck. He heard rustling below, knew they were safe, and continued holding Nigel.

In his mind, he spoke to David a little. It was hard for him to believe that his heart was light once again. Garrett knew that David would want him to live on and be happy, but that was so much easier said than done. At least he'd thought that was true, until he met Nigel, and now he felt truly alive for the first time since he'd lost David.

It was so good to just sit and hold Nigel, the late-morning sun warming his face. Garrett knew he needed to accept what happiness he got, because it was fleeting. Nigel was young, and if what he'd heard from Phyllis was correct, there was a huge wide world of possibilities and opportunities just waiting for him. As hard as it was going to be to have to walk away and let him go on with his life, Garrett would do it. Nigel deserved a chance to live on his own terms and to make his own decisions, whatever they might be.

And though they'd spent time together and had fun, he didn't expect that to translate into a lifetime together, simply because he wasn't sure if that was what Nigel wanted. Things like that only happened in stories, and Garrett knew firsthand that the stories were just that— made up to give people hope. Nothing more. He'd already experienced his story, and look how it had ended. This… whatever was happening between him and Nigel… was about as unlikely as it came. Garrett would see that Nigel and Jules got back safely and let them go on with their lives. That was the right thing to do… for Nigel.

"Do you want to go below and lie down for a while?"

Nigel shook his head. "I bet you need to, though. You were up most of the night, and if we have to leave in a hurry, you'll need to be at your best. I can't sail this without you, and neither can Jules."

"Okay." Garrett stood and let Nigel lead him below. The portholes had been opened and Phyllis had remade the beds. Nigel pointed him to the bed, and without arguing, Garrett lay down, fatigue rising almost immediately, like an undertow ready to pull him under. "Make sure everyone stays close, and keep an eye on Phyllis. I don't trust her… completely."

"It will be fine. We can sit on the deck under the cover and read or something, and I'll come get you if we see anything unusual." Nigel left, climbing out of the cabin, and Garrett closed his eyes, badly needed sleep washing over him.

The boat heaved and dipped with the rise and fall of the water, rocking and soothing him, coloring his dreams. For a while he wasn't sure what was real or dream, until the clouds around his mind lifted. Warmth pressed to him, and Garrett cracked his eyes open. Nigel lay next to him, his eyes closed, face turned to his, hair plastered to his head from the heat.

Garrett carefully slid off the bed and went topside. He blinked as he emerged into the sun. Jules and Phyllis sat in the shade, her arm around Jules. Garrett caught her eye, and she half smiled. "I'm like his mother." She wiped her eyes. "I know what I did, and I'm willing to pay whatever price for it. But I won't let anyone hurt my babies. They're as close to children as I'm ever going to get."

"But you perpetuated a lie," Garrett said. "You helped their uncle." His sense of justice screamed at him not to let her get under his skin.

"Yes, I did. At first because I was paid well. But this little guy was three years old, and…." Her words became difficult. "I'm not a monster. I tried to think of ways I could get them away."

"She did try," Jules said. "I remember once when I was young, and she told Nigel and me that we were going to go on a long boat ride." He lifted his head, blinking.

"Fairfield had taken ill, and I thought if I could get the boat keys, then I could get them away while he was gone." She stood and brushed off her clothes, probably out of nerves. "The old goat requested backup, and Hilliard sent someone else for a few days to keep an eye on things."

"Cousin Greg?" Jules asked, and Phyllis nodded. "He played toy soldiers with me."

"Yes, and if there had been anything out of place, he would have turned into a real soldier very quickly. I decided to play along, bide my time, and try to get the three of us off the island eventually. I tried twice more, but I could never get access to the boat for long enough. After that, I gave up and made sure they were safe but kept all of us as low profile as possible." She smoothed her hand over Jules's hair, her gaze hardening slightly. "I know you don't trust me, and that's fine. But while you were sound asleep, I could have taken the boat or hurt you or them if I wanted to. I also didn't say anything to the locals who were here earlier. I could have caused trouble or gotten away to call Hilliard. I didn't and I won't. I want these boys safe just as badly as you do." She put her hands on her hips, glaring at him.

Garrett stared back, neither of them backing down. "Maybe, but you're going to need to prove it to me... and to them." He turned to Jules. "I'm not telling you what to do, but remember what she did, and be careful." He didn't want to lecture him; that wasn't Garrett's place. But he wanted Jules to be able to make up his own mind and look at others with a little skepticism. He purposely said what he did in front of Phyllis, so she'd know where he stood. Then he cleared his throat before going back below. Sometimes folks were too kindhearted for their own good.

Nigel looked like he was still asleep, his nose twitching like he smelled something good, and when Garrett got close, a long arm snaked out, wound around his back, and pulled him nearer.

"What are you doing?" Garrett whispered.

"I missed my furnace," Nigel hummed softly.

"It's the tropics. You don't need a furnace here," he teased as Nigel tugged him even closer. And maybe that was the point. Nigel really didn't need him for anything. No matter what, Garrett's heart might have perked up to hope. He swallowed hard and tried not to let the dark thoughts overwhelm the others, but it was damned hard. Reality had a way of throwing its wet blanket over everything.

"I've been here for eleven years. If it gets below eighty degrees, I need a blanket." Nigel slid his arms around Garrett's waist, resting his head on his belly. "I want somewhere we can be alone. Like in the cave during the rain."

Garrett nodded and closed his eyes, remembering those few hours they'd had alone. Nothing else had mattered. Nigel had been a sweet escape from his worries, a needed diversion. At least that's what he'd told himself, knowing that wasn't completely honest but unable to face the truth.

"Do you?" Nigel asked.

Garrett nodded, unable to form words for a minute, his thoughts running jumbled through his head. "At first I wanted simple and uncluttered," he admitted. "And you represented that. We could be together and it was fun, uncomplicated, and wasn't going to last long because I was going to have to leave. But then things…." God, he had a way of not saying what he really wanted to.

"So you don't really like me… that way." Nigel's hands slipped away. "I see." He sat still, his head cocking just enough that Garrett knew he was looking beyond him. "You don't have to. I was… randy…"

Garrett smiled at his word choice.

"…and you were there, and I thought—"

"Don't," Garrett said firmly. "You don't need to say things to try to make it different than it was." He placed one hand on Nigel's head. "I didn't say I didn't like you… to use your words. It's difficult."

"Because of David?" Nigel asked.

"I thought things would be easier if I had to leave. Then I couldn't get hurt. I'd know things were temporary, that what we had was just for now. But then I kept staying. I probably should have left right away, but I couldn't. Instead, I sat around on the deck of the boat each day, waiting for you to step out of the undergrowth." Garrett smiled, and Nigel turned to look up at him. "It was like there were two sunrises each day, one in the sky and a second in my heart when I saw you."

Nigel smiled, his eyes shining. "You're a poet."

"No," Garrett chuckled. "I most definitely am not." Most of the time, he stumbled to find the right words. Lord knew he had with David.

Nigel shook his head and patted Garrett's hand. "You know what I think?" He cocked his eyebrows, and Garrett remained quiet, his gaze locked on Nigel's. "I think most men are poets when they're in love."

Garrett swallowed. "You do?" There was no way he could deny it, and if Nigel asked, he'd tell him the truth, but part of Garrett wasn't ready to say the words out loud. If he did, then they couldn't be taken back, and that led down a road he wasn't quite sure he was ready to follow. For him, those three important words had only been reserved for one person. If he said them to someone else, then he was letting go of that one connection to David and the one special, enduring link that David still had to him, the kind that death couldn't break. At least that's what the stories and love songs always said.

"I think so." Nigel sighed and held Garrett tighter. "You don't need to say anything more. I know you have troubles with saying some things." He cocked his head so Garrett could look into his eyes. "I know you aren't ready yet."

Garrett huffed softly. "And do you know that life isn't like a storybook?" he whispered, not wanting it to sound too harsh.

Nigel humphed. "And do you know that sometimes life can be a fairy tale?" He ran his hands up Garrett's back, tugging him down until he could wind his hands around Garrett's neck, closing the distance between them.

The kiss was gentle, as though Nigel knew what Garrett needed. The mind and body were already on fire, his cock throbbing in his pants, but this… it was different. It wasn't about heat or passion, but more about…. It took a second for Garrett to understand, and by then Nigel had pulled back. Garrett was being reassured, having his faith and hope rebuilt. How Nigel knew what he needed surprised and warmed him at the same time.

"It's time you got your fairy tale."

Garrett bit his lower lip. "What if I already had it?"

Nigel shook his head, rolled his eyes, and then looked at him as though he had just said the stupidest thing on earth. "We get more than one." Then, probably to silence the protest already on his tongue, Nigel kissed him again, harder and more demanding, as though to emphasize his point.

Nigel tugged him back toward the bed, and Garrett went willingly, heat building to the point that he needed to taste, feel, and smell Nigel all around him. Garrett slipped his arms under him, pressing Nigel to his chest, hijacking the kiss, plundering Nigel's mouth as Nigel stripped away his control.

Within seconds, Garrett climbed onto the bed, careful of the low ceiling, bringing Nigel along with him. He had to feel Nigel, and slipped his hand under Nigel's shirt, the kisses growing more and more urgent by the second as logical thought gave way to instinct and basic, nearly uncontrollable need.

"Nigel," Jules called from outside, a hint of alarm in his voice. "Garrett."

Garrett stopped, holding still, forcing his head to clear, even as he growled under his breath. Jules had perfect timing. Garrett slid off the bed and Nigel scampered to sit on the edge of the bed, righting his clothes, as Jules clambered down the steps.

"There are men in a boat, and they're going from group to group," Jules explained breathlessly as Phyllis joined them in the cabin.

"Do you recognize them?" Garrett asked, and Phyllis shook her head. "Okay. All three of you stay down here. Phyllis, make something for us all to snack on, please, and stay out of sight." Garrett grabbed his bag and began pulling off his clothes. "I need to put on my swimsuit so I can look like I don't have a care in the world. It isn't likely that anyone your uncle would send would know very much about me, and unless Fairfield is with them, they haven't seen me. So...." He pulled out his suit and the others turned away. He changed, grabbed a towel, and put his clothes on the bench. Then he returned to the deck, snagging an old paperback off the table as he went.

Garrett spread his towel out and grabbed his sunglasses off the console. He pretended to read his book as he watched the boat from behind his glasses. They were indeed slowly trolling around the area as though they were looking for something or someone. Garrett studied them and wished he had a way to snap pictures. Still, he committed detailed descriptions to memory, as well as the numbers on the boat and its make. They passed him without a second glance, and when they were out of sight, he called below. "They're gone."

Nigel popped his head out of the cabin. "What do we do?"

"Stay here and wait out the day. Can you grab my notebook out of the blue duffel?"

When Nigel handed it up, Garrett jotted down notes while they were fresh and continued to watch. The strangers seemed to be making another pass, so he went back to his reading, checking on any details he could add to his description. This time they came pretty close, and Garrett was able to spot an eagle tattoo on the one man's neck and what looked like part of an ear missing on the other. They were hard men who lived rough lives.

"Stay below," he cautioned without moving. "I don't know what they're looking for." He got to his feet and began stretching and moving on his towel, watching without appearing to watch. He straightened up and turned toward the boat. "Hey, guys," he called and waved, as they slowed. "Great day."

They turned his way, looked him over, and continued on without any acknowledgment. After a while, they sped off and didn't appear to be coming back.

"What was that?" Nigel asked.

"Just being a little forward. They expect their quarry to hide from them, so anyone who's out front and forward will probably be discounted." Garrett sat down and pulled open the door to the cabin so the three of them could get some fresh air. "That doesn't change the fact that you are being searched for." And it was probably best if they set sail and got away as quickly as they could.

"Can't we come out now?" Jules asked.

"Please, just stay there." Garrett wrapped his towel around his waist and went below. It was a little cramped with four people. Thankfully Phyllis had put the table up and sat on one of the bench seats out of the way. "It's for your safety."

Jules sat down, and his leg bounced. Garrett understood that he had plenty of energy and wasn't used to being cooped up like this. He and Nigel usually had an entire island to run on, and now Garrett was asking him to stay below in the cabin. "Why don't we make some dinner and try to keep busy? After we eat and it starts to get dark, we'll slip out of port and head north." Garrett pulled out his phone to check the local and regional radar, groaning.

"Is it bad?"

"Yes and no. For most larger ships, probably not. But there are some troughs of moisture and rain that seem to be heading this way. As much as I want to be able to move, we're probably stuck here at least until tomorrow." They'd have to wait for the weather to pass and any associated wind to die so the seas could calm to a safe level. Then they could venture north.

"So we have to stay here...." If there had been room, Jules would have paced.

"Just until the weather clears. Once it gets darker, you can come up on deck and sit if you want. But what if those men are looking for you?" Garrett asked, needing to be a little firm.

"Jules. This is for the best," Phyllis said calmly. "Come over here and try to relax. None of this is your fault, but remember how scared you were this morning?"

Jules hung his head slightly, nodding. "Sorry," he said softly.

"It's okay. Just be patient, and everything will be fine." God, Garrett hated giving such stupid advice, but it was all he had.

He checked the radar again, groaning softly. It would be best if they could leave now, but with the weather on the way, that wasn't safe. Additional boats would be gathering for safe harbor as well, and soon the entire place was going to be full up.

"Wouldn't anyone who's looking for us check at the harbormaster to find out which boats just came in?" Phyllis asked.

"Yes. And it'll only take a little palm greasing for them to find out that we came in last night. But they've already seen the boat and discounted us... I hope." Garrett sighed. "They don't know which direction we've gone and are going to have to check St. Lucia and even as far as Barbados by now." And the more time went on, the greater their search distance. "All we can do is not give them any indication that we're here."

"But people saw us in town," Nigel said.

Garrett nodded slowly. "I know, but unless they're willing to talk to everyone, I'm hoping that we can go pretty much unnoticed. I'm going to stay above and keep a lookout. You can help by making sure everything is straightened up and battened down here, though I don't think this weather is going to affect us much in the harbor."

"Then why don't we just leave?" Jules asked.

"The harbor is protected by the breakwater and its position. This isn't like a tropical storm or anything, but the waves on the open sea would make being out in a boat our size a difficult, rough ride. We could probably do it if we had to, but I'd rather be safe."

Nigel hugged Jules tightly. "It's going to be okay. Garrett knows what he's doing."

While Garrett was grateful for the vote of confidence, he didn't feel like he knew anything. The men he'd watched could have been looking for anyone. Hell, whoever Hilliard sent to try to find them could be closing in at this very minute. He had no idea.

Garrett went back up on deck, sat in the shade, and watched the area around the harbor as clouds thickened and the sky darkened. Most of the time, as night fell and the energy of the day left the atmosphere, the rain and storms died away, but these seemed determined. The harbor emptied of people, and the other boats rocked in the waves. Garrett went below to join the others.

Phyllis had made sandwiches, cut up some fruit, and put out a plate of crackers and cheese for dinner. It was basic but good, and they ate in silence as the first of the rain hit the roof of the cabin. It quickly grew heavier, and Garrett kept checking out the windows for any sort of activity.

"Do you see anything?" Jules asked, and Garrett backed away.

"Have a look, if you like," he offered, and let Jules peer out into the rain.

"I don't see anything." He continued around to each small window and then sat down once again. "It's strange being inside like this all the time. Even when it rained, we'd stay outside in the shelters or in the caves. When the weather was really bad, we were in the house, but this seems so small." Jules pulled at the collar of his shirt. "And it's like there's no fresh air."

Garrett opened the underside of the hatch, which let in some fresh air but kept the rain out of the interior. Jules grabbed his plate and sat nearest the opening, peering out into the rain.

Garrett wished he had things to pass the time. Searching the cabinets, he found a deck of cards, and they played for a while, until the last of the light faded. Jules insisted on sleeping on the bench by the door, and Nigel handed him a blanket. Phyllis made up the table and went to bed, which left him and Nigel with the forward cabin.

Nigel cleaned up in the small bathroom and then Garrett used it himself before climbing onto the bed and pulling the curtains in the darkness. Nigel snuggled close, and a few times Garrett felt his leg shaking. Both of them were nervous and on edge.

Garrett lay quietly, looking up at the top of the cabin just above his head, listening to the rain, feeling every centimeter where Nigel touched him. His mind raced with the desire to roll over, take Nigel in his arms, press him into the bedding, and strip him naked just so he could once again know the feel of Nigel's skin on his and know the shudder as Nigel reached his completion. That cave, rustic as it was, the sand hard under his back as he slept, seemed cozier and more inviting than just about anything he could imagine right now.

Garrett clutched the bedding with one hand as he wrapped the other around Nigel. Under normal circumstances, the rocking of the boat would easily lull him to sleep, but not tonight. He lay awake, listening to Nigel's gentle breathing and Jules thrashing around on the bench. Realizing he wasn't going to sleep, he quietly extricated himself from Nigel and slipped out of the bed. Not that he really wanted to leave, but temptation lying right next to him was more than his willpower would allow.

Jules finally settled. Garrett passed Phyllis as he grabbed an umbrella and left the cabin, then stood on the deck, watching the lights of the harbor as the rain pelted the water and decking all around him. The wind had come up, blowing around them steadily. Garrett checked the radar on his phone again and then shut it down to conserve the last of his battery. He went back into the cabin, grabbed his small bag, hoisted it under the umbrella, and left once again.

"Where are you going?" Nigel whispered from the bottom of the cabin stairs.

"Stay here. I need to go into town. I want to see if I can hear of anything strange going on."

"I want to come," Nigel said, climbing the stairs.

"Please stay here and watch over your brother and Phyllis. I won't be gone too long, I promise."

Nigel nodded, and Garrett jumped onto the dock, hoisting the umbrella, and hurried down the bouncing boards toward light and the sound of people.

CHAPTER 8

GARRETT RETURNED two hours later, having found a friendly bartender who charged his battery in exchange for a five. He moved as quietly as he could, checking for anything out of the ordinary as he made his way along the wet, sometimes slippery dock. The rain had stopped, but more promised to roll in. He reached the boat and went below. Nigel sat up as he came in, blinking and watching as Garrett toed off his shoes and slipped off his wet pants and shirt before climbing back into bed.

"What did you find?" Nigel asked.

"While I was charging my phone, I found out from the bartender that some men were here looking for two people. No one had seen them, and the men in the bar believe they left this afternoon." Garrett patted Nigel's arm. "They seemed to be looking for a man and a woman from the other side of the island who ran away to get married." He smiled.

"So those men weren't looking for Jules and me?" Nigel once again snuggled close.

"I don't know. It doesn't sound like it, but that could just be their story." In the meantime, Garrett would keep a sharp eye out and make a call to the captain with his latest information. Their luck wasn't going to hold out forever, and the more distance they put between them and the island, the more places Hilliard had to search in order to find Jules and Nigel, which only increased the chances of them getting into the country and under protection.

"Try to sleep," Nigel said.

"You too." Garrett lay down and closed his eyes, fatigue finally taking over, and he managed to fall into a light sleep, waking every hour or so.

Eventually, as light shone through the windows, Garrett reluctantly left a sleeping Nigel, checked the radar, and took a peek outside. Other boats were leaving the port, and Garrett thought now was a good time to do the same. He radioed the harbormaster, and cast off the lines, then started the engine at the last minute, guiding them out of the slip and toward the harbor entrance.

"We're leaving?" Jules asked as he popped his head out of the cabin door.

"Yes. The weather has broken and I think it's a good idea—"

Garrett quieted. Ahead, the men in the powerboat from the day before passed through the mouth of the harbor. They seemed to be watching each boat as it departed, getting pretty close to a few of them. A flash of the sun on metal told him they were armed and not afraid to show some muscle.

"Stay inside. Our friends are back," he said, turning his attention to getting the boat out of the harbor and into open water where he could be under way.

He continued forward at a reasonable pace, not wanting to look like he was rushing. As he approached the mouth of the harbor, the sleek, expensive boat swung around and came alongside.

"Hey," the man said, scowling. "You seen these people?" He flashed a picture of Jules and Nigel that must have been taken on the island about a year before.

"It's possible," Garrett said. "I was in town yesterday—lots of people there. But I might have seen those boys... maybe with a woman? She was scary, gruff, unkind."

The men looked at each other. "That's them. Did you see where they went? Someone said toward the harbor."

Garrett pursed his lips, his heart pounding a mile a minute, silently willing everyone to stay in the cabin and keep quiet. He was hoping to pull off a delicate act. "When I saw them, they looked like they'd been shopping for food. Carrying a bunch of bags and such. I thought they went farther into the city." Garrett shrugged and revved the engines, pushing the boat forward. "Sorry I can't be of more help." He waved and continued on, leaving the men to their fruitless search.

"Stay where you are," he said softly into the open cabin doorway as he continued steering.

Once free of the harbor, he turned off the engine and raised the mainsail, getting the boat under wind power. After that, he raised the jib for more speed and pointed the boat north, riding the edge of the wind.

"Okay, we're out of sight of the harbor," he called below as they rounded a bend, leaving the town behind.

Jules rushed up on deck, breathing deeply, his arms spread out as though he'd been a caged bird.

"Be careful," Nigel cautioned as Jules sat on the bow of the boat, looking forward.

"They were looking for you and Jules," Garrett told Nigel. "They had pictures of the two of you and were carrying guns. I think I outsmarted them and sent them back to the town, but I don't know." He hoped they had made it past Hilliard's dragnet, at least for now. His heart was still pounding, and it continued as they slid over the water, putting more and more distance between them and their pursuers—he hoped.

"What's the plan?" Nigel sat next to him, and Phyllis came on deck as well, sitting in the shade.

"As long as the weather and our supplies hold, we should make for the US Virgin Islands as quickly as we can." Garrett pulled out his phone and sent an email to the captain to let him know their location and plan. He wanted to get that done before he left range of the port. Then he powered off his phone, checked the GPS and radar on the boat, and pointed them in the direction they wanted to go.

"How long do you have the boat?"

"I'm supposed to turn it in at St. Thomas in a few weeks. There is a couple who want to rent it there. We have time, and that's probably the best place to contact the US authorities. So my plan was to head there." Unfortunately, if Hilliard and his goons had half a brain, they would realize the same thing and be on the lookout for them. "We all need to keep an eye out for trouble."

"We will be," Nigel said, exaggeratedly scanning the seas with his hands over his eyes.

"What can I do?" Phyllis asked.

Garrett wasn't immediately sure, and then it came to him. "Why don't you bring me my blue bag?" he said, and Phyllis retrieved it. Garrett put Nigel in charge of the wheel and dug out a tablet and a pen. "Go ahead and write up a statement of what you did for the last ten or so years, how the boys were treated, the people you saw, and what you know about Hilliard and his plans. Take your time and include as much detail as you can remember, with approximate dates. That will be a big help. Once you're done, the boys and I can witness your signature."

Phyllis took the tablet and went back below. She must have made up the beds and the table as well. Breakfast appeared a little while later before Phyllis said she was going to work on her statement.

"There are plenty of boats nearby, but none of them seems to be paying particular attention to us," Nigel said.

Garrett nodded, checking behind them. "We seem okay, at least for now." Which was a relief. Garrett had as much sail as he could, the boat slicing through the water at a good speed. Nigel sat next to him, and Garrett put an arm around his waist, tugging him a little closer.

Jules continued his fascination with the horizon, looking forward, and with Phyllis below, Garrett took a few minutes to be alone with Nigel, kissing him as soon as he turned his way.

"What did David like to do for fun?"

Garrett chuckled. "He used to drag me to art galleries all the time. David loved art and modern expression." He shook his head. "He could stand in front of a canvas of squiggly lines and see so much meaning. Me, I only saw the squiggly lines." He sighed. "David would spend hours and hours looking at pieces that hung on the walls of galleries and museums. It got to the point that I didn't go with him much any longer." That bothered him. David never really asked for all

105

that much, and yet Garrett had been too impatient, too rushed, to just spend the time with him. "I should have."

"But you didn't like it," Nigel said.

"Yes. It wasn't my thing, but it was his. And even though it meant sitting in a gallery staring at squiggly lines, I would have been doing it with him." Garrett leaned slightly against Nigel. "I miss him still."

"I miss my mom and dad. I can barely remember them now." Nigel leaned more closely. Garrett used one hand to control the boat, thankful they were pretty much headed in a straight line. They'd need to tack eventually, but for now, they were good.

"What do you remember?" Garrett asked.

"My mom was pretty. She had long blonde hair the same color as Jules's. I remember her singing to me when I was scared. She used to make up all kinds of songs for me, and at night she told us stories. Dad used to take me to the park, and he pushed me on the swings." Garrett smiled. "The last memory of my dad is him playing football with me at the park. I was really bad, but he tried to teach me how to throw, and we played catch for a long time. Then he took me to one of the carts and got me an ice cream bar." Nigel turned to him. "I don't think I've had one of those since then."

"Really?" Garrett asked.

"Yeah. We didn't have ice cream on the island," Nigel explained. "Fairfield never brought any back. Probably because it would have melted when he had it on the boat." He shrugged and grew quiet. "My dad used to love sports. I remember that. He took me to a baseball game once. The Mets won that day. Dad was so happy."

"What about your mom? What else do you remember about her?"

Nigel smiled and laughed. "Mom said she hated sports, but she went to the game with Dad and me and screamed louder than he did. Mom was out of control. She bought us all Mets shirts, then had me change into mine in the bathroom and put my old shirt in her purse. She did the same with Dad."

"Sounds like those are good memories to have. Hold on to them. It's what I do with the ones about David. I keep them in a special place in my memory so I don't lose them." Garrett smiled and figured it might be a good time to change the subject. "So, you got to see the town and go to the market on Dominica. What did you think?" There had been so much activity while they were in town, he really hadn't had a chance to ask.

"It was so busy," Nigel answered. Garrett smiled, because to him it had felt like a rather laid-back Caribbean town. "There were people everywhere, and they all seemed like they were rushing from one place to the next." He turned to Garrett. "Don't they take the time to see what's around them?"

"Most people don't." Garrett paused to think for a second. "In New York City, there is the Empire State Building. Have you seen pictures of it in your books?"

"Yes. It looks so tall."

"It is. There are ten million people who live in New York, and most of them have never been to the top of that building. Some of them see it every day and have never gone inside. You don't think about the things you see every day as being special. I live in the city, where there are tall buildings, cars and people, traffic, noise, crime, and lots of restaurants and places to see. So something like this"—he waved his arm—"being out on the water, alone, with nothing to do but listen to the wind and watch the waves roll past and on forever, that's very special to me. But it was something you saw every day."

Nigel nodded. "I suppose. But I think I'd like to see what a city looks like and ride in one of those cars. And if I go to New York, I want to go to the top of that building, so I can look out and see the ends of the world." He smiled.

"Sometimes you think you can see that far." Garrett turned to look behind them, squinting at a smudge on the horizon. He wasn't sure what it was, but it hadn't been there the last time he'd looked. At this distance, it could be a freighter or even a cruise ship, but something rankled his gut and he worried while he trimmed the lines a little, changing the sail angle to get a little more wind.

They picked up some speed according to the GPS, but Garrett had to be careful in case the waves heightened. Right now they were gentle rolling swells and the wind was steady, but it wouldn't take long for things to change. He set a course for Montserrat, bypassing French Guadeloupe, hoping to make as much distance as possible in a single day. "Can you keep an eye on that boat?" Garrett pointed.

"I will." Nigel stood and went to the back of the boat.

Garrett sailed out into the sea, and their speed continued to increase. Garrett loved the sensation of flying over the water. Under normal circumstances it made his spirit feel free, but knowing there were people out there looking for Nigel and Jules made this trip all the more urgent.

He stayed behind the wheel, and Phyllis brought him lunch. Garrett ate with one hand and steered with the other, looking back every once in a while at the boat, which was slowly drawing closer. He didn't want to tell everyone to get inside again. It was hot enough as it was, and being in the cabin would drive the others stir-crazy. Besides, if they were being pursued, it had to be for a reason, and that meant their pursuers had worked out that Nigel and Jules were on board with him.

"They're getting closer," Nigel said, tension rising in his voice. "I don't know what they were waiting for, but they're drawing closer pretty quickly now."

Garrett turned as the large, sleek cabin cruiser indeed drew steadily nearer. "Get below for safety, all of you." He leaned close to Nigel. "In the red bag in the left drawer under the bed are the guns. Bring them to me." He didn't want to panic the others, but he wasn't going down without a fight.

Nigel brought the bag and set it next to him. He let Nigel take the wheel and got the guns ready, checking the number of bullets in the magazines. He had six in one and four in the other. That wasn't a lot of firepower, but hopefully he wasn't going to need any at all.

"Check the emergency kit in the locker right there." Garrett pointed. "Is there a flare gun?"

Nigel brought out the contents, and sure enough, a case with a gun and four flares lay inside. Garrett had Nigel bring him the case, and he loaded the gun and handed it back to him.

"What do I do?"

"Nothing, and don't pull the trigger unless I tell you to. Get down in the cabin and stay near the door. I'm not going to change course and see what they do. They may just be on the same route as us and pass right by."

Nigel got in the cabin, and Garrett kept his arsenal at hand as the boat drew ever closer.

A deep voice boomed over the water. "We know you have Nigel and Jules. You are guilty of kidnapping them, and we have come to get them back."

Garrett didn't respond, and the boat drew up alongside about ten feet away. The sailboat rocked in the wake but continued forward.

"You need to lower your sails and come to a stop, or we will take more aggressive action." The men from Dominica stood on the deck, arms at their sides, trying to look intimidating. It didn't work on him.

Garrett ignored them, glancing at the horizon where the water extended forever.

The men drew weapons and the boat pulled closer.

"Give me the flare gun," Garrett told Nigel, who reached out of the cabin to hand it to him. He had the other guns, but they would be relatively ineffective against them. He needed to take the boat out of commission if he was to really get away, and a fire at sea was a sure way to make that happen. He turned his boat away from them to put distance between them.

The dark-haired man raised his gun, and Garrett figured he was going to try to take out one of the sails.

"Take the wheel," Garrett called, and Nigel jumped out of the cabin and grabbed the wheel as Garrett steadied his aim and fired a flare. It hit the top of the cabin and bounced into the water, startling the men, with one falling backward onto the deck. "Shit." Garrett grabbed another flare and loaded the gun, lowered his aim, and fired again just as a shot and a *ping* split the air.

This time his shot hit the deck of the cruiser, sending up colored smoke that filled the boat. The men dashed around, jumping like idiots, most likely because the flare bounced around the deck.

The boat veered wildly in front of him, and Garret grabbed the wheel and turned it sharply, missing the tail of the cabin cruiser by inches, the wake rocking the sailboat momentarily until the keel dug into calm water and they surged past.

Smoke came out of the main cabin of the boat, and Garrett figured the flare must have made its way inside. The cabin cruiser fell away behind them, and Garrett returned to course, once again putting distance between them.

"That was awesome," Jules exclaimed as he came on deck.

Nigel glanced back as the cabin cruiser bounced in the waves, smoke pouring out of it. "Are they going to be okay?"

"Probably." Not that he really cared, but Nigel's concern for the men who'd tried to hurt them was definitely admirable. Colored flare smoke mixed with black filled the area. It was difficult for Garrett to tell, but he thought the boat was on fire. He had other things to concentrate on, though—namely, getting everyone to port safely.

The other boat fell away quickly. He wasn't sure if they were out of commission completely or not. He sure hoped so.

"The smoke is increasing," Nigel said, and Garrett turned as a larger plume of smoke rose over the water, carried away by the wind.

"Good. Let them worry about themselves for a while." He turned back to the sea ahead of them, then remembered the *ping*. He looked up and groaned at the nick in the mast about a foot above the cabin. They were damn lucky the man was a bad shot. Either that or the boat had rocked at just the right time.

"Is everyone okay?" Phyllis asked as she came on deck, handing out bottles of water and sitting on one of the cushions in the shade.

"Yes. I think so." The excitement might have been over, but Garrett's heart was still pounding. Nigel sat next to him, shaking, and Garrett tugged him closer, giving what comfort he could.

"They really wanted to try to kill us," Nigel said softly against Garrett's neck. "They said you kidnapped us."

"You're an adult. Did you want to go with me?" Garrett asked.

"Yes," he answered, as though the question were completely stupid.

"Then you weren't kidnapped. Now Jules, that could be a different matter. He's a minor, and presumably in your uncle's care under the will. However, your uncle broke his covenant of responsibility when he tried to have Jules killed. So...." Garrett sighed and shook his head. At least he knew the kidnapping argument Hilliard was going to try to use. Now he needed to counter it....

"Phyllis, did you get a chance to finish your statement?" he asked. "I know I'm pressuring you, but we're going to need that as soon as we dock in St. Kitts tomorrow, before moving on." His plan was to call the captain and send him the statement, complete with witness signatures. "Maybe you should write a statement as well," he said to Nigel.

"Me?"

"Yes. Tell your story. How long you've been on the island, what you were told about your aunt and Fairfield. That they aren't your relatives, and you were lied to. Did you even know about your Uncle Hilliard? Explain what you knew and the kind of life you had, as well as the things you've found out since then. Just be honest. It will help complete the story we need to tell."

"Okay. Will you help me?"

"I can't. You and Jules can write it together if you like, but I don't want to influence you. Just write what you were told and what you knew. Be honest." This would give Nigel and Jules something to do other than looking behind them to see if another boat was going to try to overtake them. Garrett was doing enough worrying for all of them.

They ended up sitting on the cushions on deck, writing up their statements. It looked like some sort of demented elementary school class where they all had to stay after school to write a theme. Phyllis seemed to be doing very well, but Nigel sat with pen in hand, tongue between his teeth, as he wrote in fits and starts. It would have been adorable if he weren't struggling so much with what he seemed to want to say.

Jules sat nearby, looking out at the water, relieved that he wasn't involved in this exercise.

"I'm finished," Nigel said an hour later, handing the papers to Garrett. He read them over and asked Nigel to sign the bottom. Then he had Phyllis witness the signature, and he did the same, repeating the process with Phyllis.

"These are great." Garrett put them in his bag and stowed it carefully. "I'm going to send these to my captain as soon as we reach St. Kitts." That should be enough to rule out any sort of kidnapping charges. Now he had to get them to safety, and that might be a tall order, judging by the clouds building on the horizon.

CHAPTER 9

THE RADAR showed a growing area of rain to the east, heading toward them, but Garrett had no choice but to continue forward. They had passed Guadeloupe with crystal skies and were an hour or two away from Montserrat. Granted, there wasn't much there since the volcano had wiped out Plymouth years earlier, but the island itself would provide protection. And all he needed was to find a cove or inlet to anchor in and he could let the land shield them from the worst of the storm.

"Are we going to be okay?" Nigel asked, with Jules coming to stand near him as well. Phyllis had already gone below to put everything away in case the seas got rough.

"Yes," Garrett said, remaining positive. The tropics were beautiful, but small storms and squalls could develop almost out of nowhere because of the hot, humid air.

Clouds hung low to the water, and Garrett thought he saw land, at least at one point, but now the view was obscured and all he could do was follow the GPS maps and hope the wind didn't pick up much more. He didn't want to have to lower sails unless he had to, but it was a double-edged sword. The wind propelled them forward and was taking them to safety at the moment, but if he had to trim the amount of sail he was using, their speed would drop and they would be vulnerable to the weather for a longer time in the open water.

"Are you sure?" Nigel asked quietly enough that only Garrett heard. The boat rocked and heaved in the growing swells, sending spray up over the keel.

"I'm sure." Garrett manhandled Nigel closer. "I need you to take the wheel. I need to get the jib down." He didn't want to but had no choice. The wind continued building and the rain started pelting the roof of the cabin. "Jules, sit right here with him, and don't try to stand. Help Nigel hold the boat steady if you have too. There are life vests under the seat—put them on." He got one for himself and slipped it over his head.

Garrett climbed out of the cabin, getting soaked to the skin in three seconds. He held the grip lines, making his way forward as the bow pitched and rocked, and unhooked the jib line. He lowered it as he drew closer, securing the sail with his arms, fighting the wind that tried to billow it out once again. He had just gotten it down and was about to tie it off when a strong gust caught part of the sail. He managed to get it back under control, but his feet slipped out from under him and Garrett ended up flat on his belly on the deck, sliding toward the side, his feet dangling over the water.

He scrambled for purchase, but the only hold he had was on the sail, and it flapped in the wind. Garrett grabbed one of the lines and held on for dear life, trying to keep the sail from billowing and keep himself on the boat.

"I have you!" Nigel yelled over the wind, grabbing Garrett's hand and yanking him forward. Finally Garrett got his feet on the deck and scrambled to safety. He collected the sail and, with Nigel's help, got it tied down.

He sat, sopping wet, on the deck, one arm around the mast, the other around Nigel, eyes closed, holding Nigel for dear life as he willed his heart not to fly into a million pieces or explode in complete terror. "You saved me," he managed to say. The boat rocked less now, but Garrett wasn't able to feel his legs, so he stayed where he was and breathed, still holding Nigel.

"You scared me half to death," Nigel said as he slowly stood and guided Garrett to his feet. "We need to get back. Jules has the wheel, and we can see the island."

Garrett nodded. Nigel held the lines and scooted around the side of the cabin, climbing back under cover with ease. Garrett steadied his breath and went more slowly, dropping into the cabin and taking the wheel once again, dripping all over everywhere. He sent Jules below for safety, thanking him for all his help.

Nigel pulled off his shirt and dropped it onto the deck with a plop, but Garrett concentrated on getting them to the island. He knew there was a small town on the north side, but that didn't matter. All he really needed was shelter. Thankfully, they passed into the lee of Guadeloupe, and the rocking subsided as the winds settled. There were still waves, but they were much smaller, and as he paralleled the coast, he found a curve that formed a bay, steered them in, and dropped anchor. Finally he was able to breathe.

"Okay. We made it." He didn't want to do that again, and as soon as he stepped under the cabin overhang, Nigel hugged him tightly. Wet, warm skin plastered to him as Nigel tugged his shirt up and off and dropped it to the deck.

"You'll be warmer," he said before kissing Garrett hard, then backing away. "You saved us, twice."

"And you saved me," Garrett said, his own worry kicking in. "You could have been swept overboard."

"You almost were," Nigel retorted with a glare that quickly faded as he held Garrett tightly. "Next time you have to be more careful."

"Hopefully there isn't going to be a next time." Or another day like that. But at least they'd made it in one piece, and hopefully their pursuers were a thing of the past as well. Garrett knew sometimes he had to take risks, but today had been a number of them, and the last one he'd taken could have cost all of them their lives. It had worked out, thank God, and tomorrow hopefully they could make St. Kitts.

DINNER WAS quiet but thankfully hot. Garrett cooked a simple meal using the stove on the boat to heat up some soup and vegetables and to make noodles. It was very basic, but he had some good bread left, and at least a warm meal lifted their spirits.

The storm continued around them, the rain still pounding, but the wind died back rather quickly, which was a relief.

They were pretty much stuck in the cabin for the evening, so Garrett taught Nigel and Jules to play Hearts. After a few practice rounds, the boys blew him and Phyllis away with how they worked together.

"And you get the nasty queen," Jules said with glee as he stuck Phyllis with the dreaded card, sending her over in points and ensuring his win.

"I wonder if I should be sorry I taught them this game," Garrett teased, gathering up the cards. "Anyway, I think it's time for bed. Phyllis probably needs to sleep"—he pointed to where she sat, yawning—"and we've all had a rough day." That was the understatement of the century.

Jules nodded but didn't get up from where he sat across from Garrett and Nigel.

"I have a question," Phyllis said. "Now, I know I probably don't have any right to ask, but I'm going to anyway." She glared at Garrett. "What are your intentions with Nigel? I know you two slept in the big bed last night, and I said nothing. I know nothing... untoward happened. But...."

"Aunt Phyllis...," Nigel said without a hint of shock. "I like Garrett and he likes me." He turned to Garrett, looking into his eyes for a second. He didn't say anything more and eventually seemed to get the answer he needed. Well, it could have been Garrett's smile that did it. "Yes, he does." He grinned, and Garrett put an arm around his shoulders.

"That may be, but what are your intentions?"

Garrett cleared his throat. "My intentions are to get all of you to safety, and I'm trying not to let anyone or anything draw my attention away from that. That has to be the top priority." That sounded like the right answer, but it wasn't totally truthful. "As far and Nigel and I are concerned, we are getting to know each other. That's as far as things have gone between us, and more than you need to know." He glanced at Nigel and then to Phyllis. "I will be careful and take care of his heart as though it were my own." He took a deep breath, hoping the right words would come to him. "Nigel and Jules are going to experience a great deal of new things." He knew he was taking a dig at her, but it couldn't be helped. "Nigel deserves that chance to experience the broader world before he decides what he wants for the rest of his life. Choices have been taken away from them for too long, and as they are able to make choices for themselves, then whatever Nigel decides he wants… I'll abide by." Garret hardened his gaze and expression. "And so will you."

"Garrett," Nigel said softly.

"Nigel." He turned to him. "Part of the reason I've done all of this is so you and Jules can have choices in your life. If you decide to go back to the island someday, that's up to you. If you find you like the city and want to live there, you can choose that as well." He took Nigel's hand. "Those choices were taken away from you."

"We're kids…," Nigel said, his eyes widening in surprise.

Garrett shook his head. "You're twenty-two. You've been a legal adult for four years and should have been able to decide the kind of life you wanted to lead. That's all I want for you." He lowered his voice and leaned closer. "Yes, you've made me realize that my heart isn't dead and that I can go on after losing David." He wasn't going to talk more about what he wanted, because that didn't matter. "But what's most important is you and Jules being able to decide some things in your life." He was frustrated and a little angry at Phyllis, but tried not to let it show too much.

"But what about you and me?" Nigel asked and drew even closer. "You know, after…."

Damn, Garrett was tempted to push Nigel away a little for his own good. The words were on the tip of his tongue to tell him that what had happened on the island was a good time, but that it was best left there. That would have made things so much easier and given Nigel his complete freedom. He opened his mouth, but the words stuck in his throat. He couldn't lie, even if it might have been in Nigel's best interest.

"Like I said. You need to be given the time and the chance to make your own decisions. But you should see what the rest of the world looks like, so you know what you're deciding." He squeezed Nigel's hand.

"Okay," Nigel whispered, looking a little scared.

"Honey, Garrett is telling you that you can have what you want. And he's right. We kept you away from the world at large.

You indeed deserve to see and experience some of the world before you make any decisions about the rest of your life." She nodded, and Garrett did the same.

"But what if I know what I want?" Nigel asked.

Garrett wasn't sure how to answer that question without doing one of the things he'd told himself he wasn't going to. He was determined to let Nigel make his own decisions. "Sometimes what we want changes over time, and you should be given that time in order to know what you really want." Garrett's guts felt like they were being whipped in a blender. He wanted to see where this went with Nigel. He was such a kind, gentle man who truly touched his soul. Hell, Garrett had come alive again with a look and a touch from him.

"Is that what you want?" Nigel asked, and once again Garrett was pleased at how perceptive he was.

Phyllis cleared her throat, slipping off the bench. "The rain has stopped for now. Why don't you and I get some fresh air before bed?" She stood and opened the cabin door, then climbed out onto the deck. "Jules," she called.

Clearly Jules didn't have his brother's intuition. Still, he got the picture and followed Phyllis out.

Garrett shifted so he faced Nigel on the bench seat. "It doesn't matter what I want." Garrett had longed for a second chance, even if he'd refused to admit it to himself for a long time, but nothing came of it because he was too buried in work to allow it.

Nigel glared at him as though his eyes were laser beams. "Then you're saying that I don't know what I want?" Man, he seemed angry.

"No. I know you know your own mind. That isn't the issue." Garrett had tried to explain and was making a complete mess of it. He was trying to be selfless, but it wasn't working. "Damn it all!" He stood and took a step in one direction and then the other, hitting his head on the bulkhead that he'd successfully avoided for nearly two weeks. He swore again. "What I want is to pick you up like some caveman, carry you to bed, and have my way with you." He leaned over the table, using it to steady his arms. "I'd strip you naked and feast on every inch of you."

118

Nigel's eyes darkened and he shook slightly. "Like you did in the cave?" he whispered with a shy smile.

"Yes. But we can't do that here." Garrett sighed and cleared the fog of desire and need from his mind. He had to keep his thoughts straight if he was going to get through this... somehow. "Tomorrow we'll get to St. Kitts, and I'll call my captain. From there we'll sail to St. Thomas, and then you should be able to fly to the United States." The thought occurred to him that he'd never explained what was waiting for Nigel.

Shit.

"You and Jules.... When your father and mother died, they were very wealthy. They left everything to you and Jules, but since you were kids, they named your Uncle Hilliard"—*the bastard from hell*—"as your guardian. The thing is, once we deal with him, you and Jules will have a lot of money. You can go wherever you want and live just about anywhere you choose. The world will open up in ways you can't imagine." He took Nigel's hand, their fingers sliding together so easily.

"But...." Nigel nodded, disappointed. "You don't think I'll be good enough, with all those people."

Garrett blinked and tried to make sense of what Nigel had said, but it didn't compute. "Huh?"

"You think I won't be good enough and that when I get back, you'll find someone else who's better. You said there were lots of people, and everyone else is going to know what's going on and I'm going to be lost all the time."

Sometimes it made Garrett's head spin how a simple message could get so mixed up. "No. You're going to meet amazing, interesting, fun people, and I'm afraid you're going to find someone you like better than me." There, he'd said it. "I'm just a dumb cop." Who dared to hope for a second chance—though to prove how stupid he was, he seemed to be doing everything to screw it up.

Nigel smiled and rolled his eyes at the same time. "You're not dumb. You're brave and you saved us... all of us, twice today."

"And you saved me," Garrett whispered, trying not to think about how close he'd come to ending up in the water. God, Nigel had saved him in so many ways, and he was just starting to realize all of them. "So how about we get to St. Kitts and then beyond, and get you back into the US. From there…." He wasn't going to press anything more. "After that, you can decide what you want."

"Okay." Nigel drew him closer.

"It's starting to rain again," Phyllis said.

Garrett smiled and stole a quick kiss before Phyllis and Jules came down the stairs, closing and locking the door once again. "Then let's make up the beds and go to sleep. If this weather breaks, we'll have a busy day tomorrow."

They put everything away, and Garrett made sure that Jules had a better bed than he'd had the night before, and then he and Nigel slipped behind the curtain. With the lights turned out, for a few minutes he was able to imagine that they were all alone. That was, until Phyllis cleared her throat and coughed like she was trying to bring up a lung.

Garrett let Nigel get cleaned up and into bed before he did the same, joining him. *Temptation, thy name is Nigel.* Garrett lay on his back, listening to the snuffles as they each fell asleep. Even the rocking of the boat and the now more gentle hum of the rain couldn't lull him to sleep, not with Nigel right next to him, so near and yet so far. All he had to do was roll over and take Nigel into his arms. It was so tempting….

Just then, Nigel rolled over, his hand sliding along Garrett's belly and then along his side, holding him tightly and slipping close enough that Garrett had to stifle a groan, feeling just how excited Nigel was as well. Garrett clamped his eyes shut, throbbing against the bedding as he tried to take his mind off Nigel and the fact that his cock ached, jumping with each and every touch.

"Was it like this with David?" Nigel whispered into his ear, hand sliding down Garrett's hips and then nearer, ever closer.

"Yes and no," Garrett answered, but he wasn't going to elaborate. There were other ears too close for that kind of conversation. "Now, please go to sleep. You're going to need your rest." Hell, he needed a cold shower and maybe a block of ice to put on his dick. That seemed about the only thing that was going to cool his desire at this point.

Garrett rolled over onto his belly, shutting his eyes and trying like hell to think of unsexy things, like murder, guts, gore, or how people could be cruel to one another. And it was working until Nigel gently patted his butt and left his hand there. Garrett wanted to groan out loud, but he buried his face in his pillow and tried his best just to take his mind off all of it and go to sleep.

Whenever he really just wanted to sleep, he couldn't. His mind refused to turn off, and with walking, talking, breathing hotness lying next to him, it was impossible. Maybe he should have had Jules sleep up here and he could have crammed himself onto the bench seat. At least folding himself into a pretzel would be preferable to this torture of denial.

Nigel's hand slipped away, and he rolled over. Now Garrett could breathe somewhat again, and slowly his mind settled and he dozed off, the first time of many that night.

He woke to soft voices from the dock. Peering around the curtain, he found Phyllis's and Jules's beds empty and the cabin door closed.

"They're gone," Nigel breathed, sliding his hand down Garrett's belly and into his boxers.

Garrett swallowed the cry that threatened to erupt from his suddenly very awake and interested body. He pushed the bedding down and then turned around. Damn, he had great ideas, and as Nigel's lips slipped over him, Garrett guided Nigel's cock between his, swallowing him in a gulp, taking all of him in a haze of desire that was not going to last very long. He thrust his hips, and Nigel did the same. Garrett feasted on Nigel's flavor, taking and remembering this moment, stowing it away like one of the other precious ones so he had it when times got miserable again.

He cupped Nigel's firm butt, kneading the globes, teasing his opening with his finger, Nigel's legs shaking almost as much as his own. The days of denial and anticipation left him way too close to the edge, but with their limited time, that wasn't bad. Even though Garrett would have loved to be able to take hours together, like in the cave, that wasn't possible right now.

Nigel took him deep, sending a ripple of heat and near-control-ripping pleasure swirling through him like a tropical storm. He had so much energy and wasn't afraid to share it, and that was a huge turn-on, so much so that Garrett was already losing what little hold he had on himself. Nigel thrust, sliding his cock over Garrett's tongue, and then stilled, quivering as release racked his body. Garrett swallowed and tumbled into his own passion, holding his breath to keep from groaning out loud.

Neither of them moved, Garrett unable to and Nigel flat on top of him. He did his best to hide his panting, and eventually Nigel slipped onto the bedding, sitting up partially with a wide grin on his face that said more than a million words could possibly have.

Naughty teenagers. That was the only phrase that came to mind about what they'd done, and why did that turn him on like nothing else? It had been some years since he'd been a teenager, and Nigel had never been one in the conventional sense, so maybe this was due him. Hell, Garrett was thrilled to be part of it.

"Are they up?" Jules asked more loudly than necessary from outside, and Garrett sighed, reaching for his clothes to start dressing.

Nigel pulled on his boxers. Somehow he'd shucked them without Garrett knowing it at the time. Another talent that had definitely come in handy.

Garrett grabbed his bag of clothes and shuffled through it. "I think we'll need to do laundry in port." He was running out of clean clothes, and Nigel seemed to be as well. Those words covered the way he gazed into Nigel's eyes, pulling him closer for a deep kiss. "You were amazing," he whispered into his ear as Nigel shuddered against him. "Gather up your things and we'll get going as soon as we eat." He finished dressing and went out on deck, stretching in the morning sun and steady breeze.

"Morning," Jules said.

Garrett returned the greeting, not really in a mood to talk much. Being alone with his thoughts meant he could be with Nigel when he couldn't be there physically. "I'd like to get underway soon. That way we can hit St. Kitts for lunch, maybe find somewhere to eat, get some laundry done, and I can make some phone calls." His main hope was that they had gotten away from Hilliard's men long enough to call for help and reinforcements.

"Then I'll get busy."

"Thanks, Phyllis. Make something quick, and I'm going to get things ready here." He checked the lines and the jib to ensure it had come through yesterday's ordeal in one piece. Then he got everything rolled and stowed properly, started the engine, and pulled up the anchor. He took his place at the wheel.

He was steering them away from the island when Phyllis brought him some bread, jam, and cheese. He ate as they motored, and once he was finished, shut it down, pulled up the mainsail, and got them underway.

IT WAS a gorgeous day for sailing—the sun, the water, a steady breeze. By eleven or so, they spotted land, and by noon Garrett was on the radio arranging for a slip. A little while later, after checking with the harbormaster, they were docked and cleared to go ashore. Garrett called his boss right away and brought him up to date.

"Hilliard has very powerful friends, and he's already put out charges of kidnapping," the captain warned.

"We can put that to bed. I have a signed statement from one of the caregivers, as well as a statement from Nigel. They include the details on the attempt to try to kill them, and the attack on our boat as we tried to get away. I'm going to send them over." He set the pages out on the table, took a photo of each one, and sent them via email. He also emailed them to himself for safekeeping. "You can see they were all witnessed properly. He may try, but four of us can attest that the statements were properly given."

"Perfect." Garrett could almost hear the smile on the captain's face. "I'm going to send these over to a contact at the DOJ. They have been after this guy for a while. His business practices have skirted the law for some time. This may be enough to get him charged, but we're going to need each of them to testify in order to make this stick."

"I know." Garrett was relieved when the last image sent. Then he gathered up the pages and slipped them back into the plastic bags, sealed them inside another, and hid them deep in the boat. "The statements have been double sealed, so even if we sink, they should survive." He went on to describe the earlier attack.

The captain laughed hard. "You flare-gunned them? Damn, I would love to have seen that."

"I had the guns I got on the island, but I needed to incapacitate the boat so they wouldn't follow. That seemed like the best way. I honestly don't know what happened to them. They might have caught fire and gone down for all I know or care."

"That's harsh," the captain said. "More like the Wreckley I know."

"They've tried to kill Jules and Nigel and then they chased us down, shot at us, and threatened both of them again. They got whatever was coming to them, and so will Hilliard." Garrett needed to bring this to an end.

"Yes, definitely. The Justice Department got a handle on their parents' will, and since Nigel Montague is of age, he can claim his inheritance, as well as guardianship of his brother. That was stipulated in the will. That will strip most of Hilliard's assets and power. But we need to get them to New York to do it. That's where the will is registered, so that's where they need to make their case."

"Okay. As I said, we're in St. Kitts now, so hopefully we can make St. Thomas in a few days. Have you made any headway on their identification?"

"Get them to St. Thomas. Justice will have someone there with the documents they need. The big thing is to get them there as quickly as possible, and unfortunately they have to arrive by boat because there is no airport anywhere that will let them fly."

"We'll plan to leave soon, as long as the weather holds." A few more days with Nigel, and then the rest of the world would intrude. Garrett had been lucky to have Nigel pretty much to himself for as long as he had. Still, he hated the idea of sharing Nigel with anyone, let alone the entire world. He actually wished he could delay the trip just to spend more time with Nigel, but that would only put them in danger, and Garrett wasn't going to do that.

The captain ended the call. Garrett had his marching orders.

Garrett put his phone in his pocket and took a deep breath of sea air.

"You done with your calls?" Nigel asked. "We want to go to town or something. I think you said we could eat here."

"Yes. We'll find a restaurant and see about laundry and supplies." Garrett glanced around. "We have to get what we need and leave as soon as we can. My captain has made arrangements, but we need to get to St. Thomas. That's going to take us a little while longer, and the sooner we get there, the safer you are going to be." And the closer Garrett was to heartache. "Let's stow everything and go on into town."

"I put together a bag of laundry," Phyllis said, hefting it.

They climbed off the boat and down the floating dock to their first dry land in days. It took Garrett a while to stop feeling the rocking of the sea under him. The others seemed to have the same trouble, but they quickly got into town and the sensation faded. They found a local restaurant and went inside. The scent was a party for the nose, and the food, when it came, was stunningly good.

"I like this," Jules said, taking a big bite.

"Fairfield wasn't as good a cook as he liked to think he was," Nigel commented. It was the first time anyone had mentioned him in a while. "I wonder if he ever got away or...." Nigel didn't finish his thought, and Garrett figured it was probable that Fairfield wasn't among the living.

CHAPTER 10

ST. THOMAS was in sight, just close enough to come into cell phone range. Garrett called the captain and got an immediate answer.

"What the hell took you so long?" the captain groused. "I was expecting you there yesterday, and I've been wondering if you were sent on a wild goose chase through the city."

Garrett shook his head. *What the hell?* "We ran into weather and—"

"Steve, look. I'm working right now and can't talk. Let me call you back when I finish with this meeting."

The call went dead, and Garrett shoved his phone in his pocket with more force than was necessary. He held the boat in a fairly steady position, outside the entrance channel, as he waited. Nigel sat next to him with the others on deck, looking out at the collection of hills that made up the lushly green island.

"Can we go dock now?" Jules asked, but Garrett shook his head. He wanted to wait to hear what arrangements had been made before he walked into a potential hornets' nest. The last thing he wanted was to dock and then get thrown in jail for kidnapping, and for Nigel and Jules to end up in the hands of their uncle anyway. To pass the time, he decided to give Nigel and Jules a lesson in sailing against the wind. By skating the edge of the wind, it was possible to sail against it, though it required a zigzag pattern and a lot of tacking.

Finally his phone buzzed. "Sorry about that. The chief was in here. There are rumors running through certain circles about Nigel and Jules—possible kidnapping, etcetera—most of them started by their uncle, I'm sure. He isn't happy."

"Does he know I'm involved?" Garett swallowed. This could end his career with the force.

"Not for certain. But I think he suspects. You were supposed to be on vacation and out of the spotlight... remember?" He paused as though he were giving Garrett a chance to think things over. "Justice will have a representative meet the boat. His name is Carver Milne. It's possible that their uncle has worked out where you're going to come in, but hopefully not when. The idea is to get them from the port, verify who they are, and take them to the airport, where a private plane will take them to New York." The captain cleared his throat. "You've done an amazing job with this and done those boys a real service. Once they're on the plane, continue with your vacation, such as it is. And I'll see you back in Baltimore."

"But—"

"I have more visitors headed my way and have to go." He cut off the call, and Garrett damn near threw his phone into the ocean, he was so frustrated and pissed off.

"Is it bad?" Nigel asked, and Garrett reminded himself that his frustrations weren't Nigel's and Jules's and he needed to keep it under control for them.

"It's okay. Someone is going to meet you in St. Thomas, and they're going to take you the rest of the way back to New York." Garrett managed to keep his voice from breaking, but just barely. He'd known this day was coming, and now that it was here, he was tempted to turn the boat around and sail back out to sea just so he could have a few more days with Nigel.

Nigel's eyes narrowed to slits. "You aren't coming with us?"

Garrett sighed, trying to find the words to explain. "I'm supposed to be on vacation and... no one knows that you and I...." He slipped an arm around Nigel's waist. "Things could get complicated if they found out how close we were.... No." He wanted to go along, though, and would have thrown his mother in front of a raging bull to get to go with them. "This trip seems to be invitation-only." The justice department did things their way.

Nigel slid off the bench, stood a few steps away, and glared at him, hands on his hips. "You could come if you wanted to."

Garrett wasn't so sure of that. "You need to go back and claim what is rightfully yours." He reached for Nigel, but Nigel took another step back and nearly fell over a line. "There's more than just the four of us involved now. These people will look after you and keep you safe. They're also the people who will see to it that your uncle pays for what he tried to do to you. They can help you a lot more than I can now." Garrett's time in this story was coming to an end. He could feel it, the same darkness that had enveloped him after David's death threatening to spread once again. It had been held at bay by Nigel for days, and he'd actually thought it might have been gone for good, but it was back, and growing once more. "I won't let you go with anyone until I know you're safe."

Nigel bit his lower lip, blinking and just staring. "You are so full of seagull shit, it isn't funny." Finally, he moved closer. "You saved Jules, and me, a ton of times. Heck, you set a boat on fire with a flare gun to keep us safe, and you're going to be put off by this Justice guy, whatever he is?" The fire in Nigel's eyes flared and then dimmed. "Maybe you aren't the kind of man I thought you were." And maybe Nigel was right.

Garrett sighed and steered the boat into the mouth of the harbor and toward the slip where he had agreed to leave the boat at the end of his vacation. Yes, he was there much earlier than he'd intended, but it was empty. Hell, maybe after dropping off Nigel, Jules, and Phyllis, he'd get back on the boat and go wherever the wind took him for the rest of the time he had.

He threaded through the busy harbor opening, waiting for a cruise ship to maneuver into place before searching for the slip he was supposed to use. It took a few minutes before he changed course and found what he was looking for. He turned to the others. "You all go below. I don't know what kind of reception we're going to get, and it's better safe than sorry right now."

Nigel and Jules crossed their arms over their chests and shook their heads. Even Phyllis stood her ground.

"We'll face whatever fate we have to out here." Nigel swallowed. "I'm tired of cowering."

"Okay." What else could he say to that? Garrett started the trolling motor and handed the wheel over to Nigel, while he and Jules lowered the sails and secured them.

"Do you really think it's going to be okay?" Jules asked.

"I hope so." Garrett didn't have a lot of false hope to give.

Jules nodded. "Will we see you again?" He helped stow and secure the mainsail.

"Count on it." Garrett patted Jules on the shoulder. "I'll sail with you and Nigel anytime, anywhere." He swallowed and turned away to secure the last of the sail.

"You really—" Jules paused and turned back to where Nigel steered the boat slowly forward. They were basically staying still, which was perfect. "You love Nigel, don't you?"

Garrett wasn't going to confirm to Jules something he hadn't told Nigel, so he patted the sail and returned to the wheel. "Let me take it from here," he said gently, and maneuvered the boat the last way into the berth.

Jules secured the lines as a man strode along the dock in light pants and a white shirt.

"Mr. Wreckley," he called, and Garrett turned, motioning Jules back onto the boat. "I'm Carver Milne from the US Justice Department. I believe you were expecting me." He showed Garrett his identification.

Garrett relaxed. "Yes, I am. This is Nigel and Jules Montague, and the lady is Phyllis Righton. And yes, we were expecting you." He shook Carver's hand and motioned him on board. "Do you have the documentation they need?"

"Yes." Carver opened a satchel and pulled out two sets of pages and handed them over. Garrett looked at them and then passed them to the boys. "These will allow you to get on the plane and through customs and immigration on the other side."

"What do we do then?" Nigel asked, his confidence slipping away and the inexperienced, though now scared, person Garrett had met on the island coming forward once again.

"I'm going to take you to the airport, where we have a plane that's set and ready to take all three of you back to New York," Carver said in an official, detached tone. "From there we have people who will provide for your safety."

Nigel nodded. Then he looked at Garrett. "Will you come with us?"

"I'm sorry, but—"

"Yes," Garrett interrupted, flashing Carver a dirty look. "I'll go with you." The least he could do was see to it that Nigel and Jules made it all the way to the plane, and then he could watch it take off and carry them away. "Let's get your things and button up the boat." He wasn't giving Carver the chance to argue with him.

Jules went below first, with Phyllis following. Nigel's shoulders slumped, and he went as well a few seconds later.

"There isn't a lot of room in the car and—"

"Nigel and Jules have been through a lot, including attempted murder. So try to understand if they want someone they know around them." Garrett stepped into Carver's personal space. "Try to be a little understanding." He crossed his arms over his chest and waited for the others.

"We're ready," Nigel said, standing next to Jules, each holding the duffels Phyllis had packed for them on the island. Phyllis came up with her bag. Garrett got the papers and things he'd hidden earlier, closed up the boat, and they all filed off the boat, down the dock, and toward the parked cars.

Carver led them to a black sedan. He stowed the luggage in the trunk, and they all climbed inside. Phyllis sat in back with the boys, and Garrett rode up front with Carver.

Garret had forgotten that on St. Thomas, they drove on the left side of the road, which was unnerving since most of the cars had the wheel on the left side. Garrett couldn't figure out how they could see to drive, and the absence of a lot of side mirrors on the cars spoke to the fact that many couldn't.

"It's okay, boys," Phyllis said as they both leaned on her.

Garrett turned away and watched out the window as his own emotions rose to the surface.

"There's nothing to be worried about. We have—" The driver's side window shattered and the car swerved. Carver gasped and grabbed his arm. "Shit." Blood spilled out from under his fingers. "I've been shot."

"Pull over," Garrett said as the car weaved from side to side on the narrow road. Carter did, and Garrett got out as another shot rang through the air, shattering one of the rear windows. "Everyone, get down!" Garrett raced around the back of the car and jumped into the driver's side as a bullet whizzed by his ear, with Carver sliding into the other seat. Garrett yanked the door closed and floored the accelerator. The wheels spun before digging in and propelling them forward. He clutched the wheel, fighting his instincts to move to the right side of the road as he went as fast as he dared.

"There's someone behind us," Jules said.

"Stay down. Carver, call for some help and tell me how to get to the damn airport."

Garrett continued along the road, climbing into the hills. Carver explained that he needed to turn left in about a mile, then got on the phone as the car behind them tried to ram the back. Garrett sped up, nearly skidding to the side as he took a curve, checking the rearview mirror. The car behind them fishtailed, slamming into the inner rock face, bouncing off, and nearly careening down the side of the mountain. Garrett didn't stop as he put distance between them.

"We're under fire," Carver said. "I think we lost them, but I've been shot, and we need to get these people on the plane and away as soon as possible."

Jules groaned as Garrett took a corner as fast as he dared, following Carver's directions out toward the airport.

"Can you slow down?" Phyllis asked.

"I wish I could. Carver needs help, and you need to get to the airport. Just hang on and I'll get you there as fast as I can." All he could think about was getting Nigel and Jules to safety once again.

"Take this right. It's the back entrance. Our plane is parked just beyond the hanger over there." He gritted his teeth in pain. "Just get there."

"We need to go to a hospital," Nigel said.

"I'll get this taken care of once you are all safe." Carver turned to Garrett. "Just get us to that plane."

Garrett turned in and braked to a stop at the security checkpoint. Carver did the talking, and they continued on and pulled up to a Gulfstream jet.

Two men stood at the entrance. They hurried to the car and presented their identification.

Garrett got the bags from the trunk, then helped Nigel and Jules to the steps into the plane.

Nigel stopped at the top. "I'm not going anywhere," he said loudly, hurrying back down. "Unless you come with us." He grabbed Garrett's hand. "I know there isn't time, but we need you. We both need you, and I don't trust anyone else. Not after all this." Nigel pulled him up the stairs, and Garrett was powerless to stop him.

"Get in," Carver echoed from inside. "We have to go. Now!"

Garrett followed Nigel inside, took the seat next to him, and barely had a chance to fasten his seat belt as the attendant pulled the door closed. The plane engines started and revved, the plane taxied to a runway, and soon they were in the air, climbing quickly and steeply. Only then did Garrett dare to release the breath he'd been holding.

"Nigel, you and Jules are going to be fine," Carver said from the seat across the way. A man in the chair next to him looked at his shoulder.

"You were lucky. The bullet went through pretty cleanly. I'm going to bandage you up, and when we land, we'll have doctors there to get you to a hospital." He finished bandaging the wound and fit Carver for a sling.

Garrett turned to Nigel, took his hand, and squeezed it. He hoped Carver was right, but Garrett had a feeling they had just gone from the frying pan into the fire, and there wasn't a damn thing he could do about it now.

JULES YAWNED and spread out across two of the seats. One of the FBI agents accompanying them found a blanket and pillow, helping to make him comfortable.

Phyllis had put her feet up and reclined her seat, closing her eyes.

Garrett leaned against Nigel, yawning. "It's been a very active and busy week." They were all tired.

"Do you need anything to drink?" Carver asked, pointing. "Tell Jenkins here and he will get whatever you need."

"Why don't you get Nigel and me a Coke? That would be great." Garrett sat back, trying to still his racing thoughts.

"I remember those from when I was a kid."

Jenkins brought two cans. Garrett opened them and handed one to Nigel, who drank too fast and burped loudly. Then he drank more slowly and smiled.

"This is good."

"Haven't you had Coke before?" Jenkins asked.

"Not in a really long time." Nigel drank some more and burped softly.

Garrett let Nigel finish his drink, then undid his seat belt and went to the front of the cabin. Nigel joined him, leaving Phyllis and Jules to rest, as did Jenkins and Carver, the agents sitting across from them. "Nigel deserves to know what you're planning," Garrett said, meeting their steely gazes. "As you saw firsthand, their uncle will stop at just about nothing to keep these boys from returning home to claim what's rightfully theirs."

"We have notified their parents' law firm that the boys have been located and that Nigel is of age. They have prepared court documents and have all the required procedures ready to go once Nigel presents himself."

"But what about my uncle?" Nigel asked.

"The people who chased you in St. Thomas were apprehended and are being questioned, or will be once they get medical attention. It seems their car went off the embankment. They survived and are in federal custody on the island," Carver said after checking his phone. "We will use that information, along with the statements that have been provided, to bring charges against him in federal court." He winced as he sat back. "I have been after something on that man for years now." Carver didn't look much older than Garrett, but he might have been gifted with good genes.

"Do you know what happened to the men who chased us in the boat, or Fairfield and the men on the island?" Nigel asked.

"We don't know about the boat, but...." Carver turned to the agents, who began typing on computer keyboards—either requesting information or taking notes, Garrett wasn't sure. "The others were reportedly found." He swallowed, his gaze alternating between the two of them, and Garrett knew that was his way of saying they were dead while trying not to upset Nigel. "We suspect the others met a similar fate."

Nigel lifted a nail to his lips and bit it nervously. "Uncle Hilliard will stop at nothing...."

"That's true. And he isn't going to leave anyone to testify against him if he can help it." Carver's hard expression told Garrett he understood just how important and dangerous this whole situation was.

"How big is his organization?" Garrett asked.

"Well, there's the manufacturing and corporate interests that were the basis of his fortune. Actually, those are what Nigel and Jules will inherit. They have boards of directors and other shareholders that have kept Hilliard from truly corrupting them. What he has done is take the money he got from running those and use it to further his own private interests, and it's those that cause us the most concern. He doesn't care who he hurts or what he has to do in order to get what he wants."

That was worse than Garrett had figured. "It seems he likes to get his hands dirty."

"Yes. He likes to be feared. Oh, and he's smart. Witnesses disappear and end up dead. He doesn't leave loose ends. Until now." Carver's eyes flicked to Nigel, and a chill went up Garrett's spine.

"I'm not a loose end," Nigel said firmly. "I'm his nephew." He set his jaw for a few seconds and then turned away. "Even if he's never seen us the entire time he was supposed to have been caring for us." Nigel grew rigid. "He only wanted us out of the way."

"And alive…," Carver said clearly. "Your parents' will is very specific. Everything goes to you and your brother, but without you two, it goes to a charitable foundation. So he needed to keep you alive, at least for a while."

"Then why kill them now?" Garrett asked, gathering Nigel closer. He hated that he had to ask these questions in front of him, but then Nigel needed to know the truth about who they were up against. He wished he could take it away and bring Nigel back to that cave where it would be just the two of them again.

"We believe that the boys had started to become a liability some time ago."

"Yes," Phyllis said as she came over, taking an empty seat. "Fairfield was getting edgy and nervous, and I think that's because Hilliard was as well. He had people in the village who reported to him, and when you went there and started talking to people and asking around, he nearly went out of his skin."

Garrett groaned. "So I'm the reason he sent people to hurt them?" The thought stabbed at Garrett's heart.

"Yes and no. Nigel is an adult now. Hilliard knew that, and so did Fairfield. They thought it would be only so long before Nigel wanted to leave the island, and once that happened, he'd figure out who he was. The whole situation would unravel." She laid her folded hands on the table. "Fairfield was starting to suspect I wasn't going to go along." She turned away and wiped her eyes. "I couldn't. Nigel and Jules were my family and have been for years. I kept them on the island to keep them safe. Hilliard would have hurt them if they left."

"I know that now," Nigel said softly as Garrett nodded. He had little doubt that she was telling the truth.

"But why kill them now if he gets nothing?" Garrett asked.

Carver shrugged, and Jenkins took a deep breath. "We have a theory. With the boys dead, a will could be found at the last minute leaving everything to their beloved uncle. I suspect a fake will is locked away in a safe or strongbox somewhere and has been sitting there for years now, ready for when it was needed." Jenkins turned to Nigel. "No one has seen you in over a decade, and any questions about your welfare were squashed or paid to go away."

"So my presence in part brought this whole thing forward?" Garrett asked, and the others nodded. He'd also put Nigel and Jules in danger. If he'd minded his own business....

Garrett swallowed hard and tried to push the guilt away. It was useless, and truthfully, Hilliard would never have allowed the boys to inherit anything. This had been going to happen eventually. All he'd done was save their lives. He kept reminding himself of that.

"All right." Nigel's voice sounded firm. "You believe that the core businesses, the ones my father owned and belong to us, are sound and...."

"Legit? Yes. They have had regular audits by outside, nationally known firms. In one case the board moved to limit your uncle's authority, taking more direct control," Carver said. "And your uncle now has his own money."

"Then why does he care about Nigel and Jules?" Garrett asked.

Jenkins stood and wandered through the cabin before returning to the table. "If he didn't have the legitimate businesses to provide him some sort of credibility, he couldn't do his other deals." He shifted his weight like he couldn't settle. "Trying to get in this man's head... it's nearly impossible and ugly."

Garrett didn't doubt that. "So what's the first step?"

Jenkins sat back down and turned to Nigel. "We'll get your parents' attorneys to certify that you and Jules have claimed your inheritance. I suspect that will make national news, and that's good. It means you aren't being hidden in the shadows, and that gives you some safety. We are also assuming that you will want to claim guardianship of Jules, removing it from your uncle."

"Yes," Nigel answered firmly, squeezing Garrett's hand under the table until Garrett thought his fingers would break. "But I don't know anything about running a business or what my parents had." He turned to Garrett, his expression lost, his eyes filling with fear. "I can't do this alone. I just can't."

Garrett wished he knew what to say. "Take one thing at a time."

Nigel nodded, biting his lower lip nervously. "Where does my uncle live?"

"In a penthouse in midtown Manhattan. It was your mom and dad's home. He moved in after they died and has lived there ever since."

"Do you remember it?" Garrett asked.

Nigel paused. "Yeah, I think so. It was a long time ago, but there are things I remember. It had a private elevator, and Jules used to love to go for a ride. So I used to take him up and down in it three or four times a day." Nigel smiled and looked over at his sleeping brother. "We each had our own room and a play area with toys, and there was a rooftop garden and terrace. I used to play out there all the time. There were these stone walls that looked like battlements, and I used to make believe that the terrace was my castle."

"That apartment is part of your inheritance," Carver said. "So you and Jules can live there again if you want to kick your uncle out." He smiled and then winced as the plane shook from a little turbulence. "We've wanted to get in there for a long time and got close on a couple of instances, but never managed to get quite enough evidence to get a warrant."

Garrett grinned. "Maybe you won't need one." He raised his eyebrows. "Since the owners are right here, they could give you permission to search the apartment. After all, he has no right to the estate or any of its assets and is living there illegally. The apartment has belonged to Nigel since his twenty-first birthday." He glanced at

Nigel. "What do you think? That would be a great way to meet your uncle and possibly get additional evidence on him. Get a look at his personal files, everything he's got there."

Carver made a few notes, and Jenkins typed on his computer, probably messaging back to the department. "Yes. That's a go. We can only do that once they have claimed the estate, and then we can go to help Nigel enforce his claim. If he invites us in and allows us to look around, we can do that since at that point he will own the property and has by right owned it since he was twenty-one." Carver was smiling at that point.

"What do you think?"

Nigel nervously shifted his weight in the chair. "He's my uncle… family…."

Phyllis took his hand. "Remember what he did and tried to do." She blinked and turned away to wipe her eyes. "That man is evil to the core. Have no doubt about that. This penthouse belonged to your mom and dad. He doesn't deserve to live there, and has conspired to keep you away from it. Don't be kindhearted where he's concerned." She knew him so well. Garrett nodded his agreement.

A scream split the air. It chilled Garrett's blood and sent him to his feet.

Jules screamed again, and Garrett raced over to him and gently lifted him into his arms. "It's all right."

Nigel joined him, trying to soothe Jules as he clutched at Garrett, practically clawing at him. "Jules, wake up. It's just a dream."

Jules slid his eyes open and blinked, shaking in Garrett's arms.

"Is he okay?" Phyllis asked as she tried to get to him. Jules held Garrett so tightly, Garrett knew he was going to have marks.

"He will be. Let's give him some air," Garrett said gently as Jules continued to wake up. "You're okay. It was just a dream."

Jules closed his eyes again, still quivering in Garrett's arms.

"Jules, I'm here," Nigel soothed, and Jules nodded but continued clinging to Garrett as though he were a lifeline.

"What happened?" Garrett asked gently.

"I was alone and people came to take me," Jules said. "I don't remember a lot of it."

"That's okay." Garrett was pretty sure that the last few days, with the running and being chased and the shooting in the car, were all mixed up in Jules's mind, complete with losing the people he'd thought cared about him. Garrett was shocked he hadn't been having nightmares before this. "You're safe now, and Nigel and I, along with these agents, are going to do our best to see that you stay that way." He helped Jules to sit back down.

"Are you hungry?" Carver asked, and one of the two other agents, who had been sitting near the door the entire time, went into the galley area and returned with plates of sandwiches, spreads, veggies, and fruit. She set the plates on the table, along with the silverware and glasses, before returning to her place.

Garrett gave up his seat to Jules and grabbed a few sandwiches, and went up to sit in a forward seat.

"Thank you," Nigel said, plopping into the seat closest to the window, looking out as the earth passed beneath them. He leaned close, whispering into Garrett's ear. "Jules is having a hard time with all this, but he doesn't want anyone to know. I think he's embarrassed, and…."

"There's no need to be," Garrett whispered back more coolly than he intended, but things were quickly closing in around him. He wanted to help Nigel and Jules, he did, but the more he did, the more they relied on him and… the harder it was going to be on all of them when he was forced to go back to his own life. "He's been through a lot. You both have. I'm surprised both of you haven't had nightmares long before now." He sure as hell would have.

"I probably will, but I haven't had a chance to think about it." Nigel snatched a sandwich off Garrett's plate, so Garrett handed the whole thing over, got up for another one, and brought back a couple of sodas as well.

Nigel spent a lot of time looking out the window as he ate, and Garrett left him alone. After a while, Garrett returned to the table at the back of the plane where the agents were talking softly, passing Jules, who was now asleep again, sitting next to Phyllis.

"Do you know how you want to handle this with their uncle?"

"I think so," Carver said. "I won't be able to be there, though I'd really like to. I'm probably going to need to spend some time at the hospital...."

Garrett leaned over the table. "I think we arrange for hotel rooms in a public place, somewhere that's really nice. Let them have some time in a fresh, clean, nice bed to rest. The lawyers can visit them there and take care of things. We can confront the uncle as soon as you're ready. I'd like you to be there. After all, the guy had you shot, so you should at least have the chance to slap the cuffs on him." If Garrett were in Carver's place, he'd want a chance for a little poetic justice.

"All right." Jenkins was already working, and Garrett peered around the computer. "How about this one?" He showed Garrett one of the large high-rises on Times Square. "This will be good." He smiled and checked rooms. "There are suites on the top floor with restricted access. I can get three rooms on that floor. We can provide security. Let me call the hotel." He stood and walked to the galley, talking softly, and Garrett returned to Nigel.

"This is my first time in a plane since I was a kid. Mom and Dad took me to Disney when I was seven." His lips turned upward and his smile warmed. "Dad arranged for us to have lunch with some of the characters. I remember dancing with Winnie-the-Pooh." Nigel chuckled. "That was the last time I flew anywhere, except for when they brought us to the island." He shook and after a minute turned decidedly green.

"It's okay. Do you want something to drink?" Garrett gently patted Nigel's arm. "Breathe deeply."

"They brought us there on a plane that lands in the water, and it was awful." Nigel took deep breaths and slowly his color returned to normal. "I was sad, and Jules cried all the time. He wanted Mommy. So did I, but they were gone." He continued breathing evenly and deeply. "I miss them still."

"Of course you do." How could Nigel not miss his parents? "But you're not alone." Dammit, he wasn't going to abandon them.

The plane shook, and Garrett's ears popped.

"We are about a half hour from the New York area and have started our descent," the captain said.

Garrett made sure Nigel and Jules were seated with their seat belts fastened while the others cleared the table and took care of their papers.

On the ground, they were met by a black limousine. Their luggage was transferred to the back of the car, and soon they were rolling toward the city.

"Isn't this a little conspicuous?" Garrett asked.

"Nope. This is New York, and I figure if Hilliard is searching for his nephews here, he isn't going to expect them to arrive in a limousine. The decoy convoy of black SUVs with lights flashing is way more noticeable." Carver sat back.

Once they arrived at the hotel, they were shown directly to a private elevator and whisked high into the sky. Carver had stayed in the limousine and promised to get medical care.

"Is this where we're staying?" Jules asked. He raced into the room and landed on the huge sofa with a bounce. Then he got up and hurried to the windows, leaning close to the glass. "It's really high up... and all those lights." He turned away. "It's going to be so bright. How do we sleep... and the noise?" He put his hands over his ears. To Garrett, it didn't seem like much, but he listened as the muffled sound of the city intruded through the windows. To someone who had only ever heard the ocean as white noise, this must be unnerving.

"Where are we going to live?" Nigel asked before setting down his and Jules's bags.

"That's up to you." Thankfully, the agents had gone to their room, while some stood guard out in the hall, and Phyllis had her own room next door, which had had the phone removed and was secured. There were two bedrooms in the suite.

"I get this one," Jules called as he raced into what was undoubtedly the master bedroom.

"I think you can have the one over there on the other side of the room, and Garrett and I will sleep in here," Nigel corrected. "Unless you want to sleep on the sofa."

"Nope." Jules took off toward the other room.

"At least carry your bag."

Jules raced back, suddenly a barrel of energy, grabbed the bag, and ran off.

"I don't remember him this wound up before," Garrett commented.

Nigel nodded. "I think the close quarters we've been in are starting to get to him." He placed his bag on the floor of the bedroom.

Garrett didn't have anything. All his stuff was still on the boat, a thousand or more miles away.

"Can we go out and see things?" Nigel asked as he wandered over to the window.

"I don't think so, not today. The lawyers are coming in an hour, and then I'll have dinner brought to the room. You can watch television if you want." He showed Nigel how to use the remote, turning on the television.

Nigel stared at the screen for a few minutes and then turned it off. "It's so noisy and—I don't know the programs." He made a face, relaxing as soon as the room was quiet again. "Are there books?"

Jules came back in and bounced as he sat on the sofa. "I can see the ocean from my window." He bounded up again, and Nigel went after him.

Garrett tried to explain that they were glimpsing the Hudson River, but they were gone. So he picked up his phone and called the agents in the other room.

"Is there an issue?" Jenkins asked.

"Is it possible to get us a couple of iPads? I can give you a credit card. The guys are bored and need something to do." He was sure Nigel would reimburse him.

"Can't they watch television or something?" Jenkins asked.

"They haven't watched much television in eleven years. It's noisy to them. Remember, they lived on an island away from everyone else. Just have someone go get a couple of iPads, please. I can set them up for them. They want to read, and I think that having a ton of books at their fingertips is a good idea." Garrett got a noise of agreement and ended the call.

The boys were still in the bedroom, standing at the window.

"What's that building over there?"

"The Chrysler Building. And right over there is Grand Central Station. I think if you look out the window in the other bedroom, you can see the Statue of Liberty. The Empire State Building is right there." He pointed out each landmark.

"How do people know where they're going? There are so many buildings and roads and cars. So much to remember." Jules's mouth hung open, and Garrett could almost see him trying to equate this place to what he knew on the island. "There aren't any trees, and there's no real ocean, just a fake thin one over there and...." His shoulders slumped. "Nigel, I want to go home."

Garrett's heart broke. Even Nigel seemed nervous and uptight. "After we take care of your uncle, I'm going to show you the subway and take you up on one of those tall buildings so you can see everything. We'll show you all around the city. And I can take you to Central Park. It's filled with trees and water, a pond, and we can go out in a boat."

"Okay," Jules agreed, turning back to the window.

"And as for how people get around, they use their phones." Garrett pulled out his and brought up the map. "You can put in the address of where you want to go, and it gives you directions. We'll get you each a phone of your own, I promise." Heck, he'd get them whatever they wanted if it made them more comfortable.

A soft knock on the door drew his attention, and Garrett left the room to answer it.

"Here you are," Jenkins said, handing Garrett a bag from the Apple store.

"Thanks."

"We got a call from the lawyers' office. Someone will be here soon. We'll check them out and bring them up when they arrive."

"We appreciate it." Garrett closed the door, sat on the sofa, and opened each of the boxes to get the devices charging while he set them up. Garrett added both devices to his account and hooked them up to the hotel's Wi-Fi, then downloaded a reading app to each.

"Guys, I have something for you." He called them in and showed them how to work the iPad to read books. "What do you want to read?" Garrett asked each of them, and he downloaded their favorite books. Soon Nigel was curled on the sofa, the iPad on his lap, reading away, even smiling.

Garrett showed Jules how to use the internet and play various games, and soon he was engrossed in Candy Crush. Garrett sat on the foot of the sofa, Nigel's feet in his lap, with the television on low, watching a rerun of *The Nanny*.

Time seemed to fly by, and soon enough the lawyer, Keller Phipps, arrived, wearing a gray suit and red power scarf, with a perfect, conservative haircut. She looked about twelve. Jules stayed in his room with his new pastime, and Garrett and Nigel sat at the table with the lawyer. Nigel handed her the identification papers that they'd been given and answered a number of questions.

"I'm sorry for all that, but I had to be sure it was you," Keller said as she opened her case. "My father originally drew up the will, and he knew your parents very well. Your dad was one of his closest and dearest friends. He's so disappointed that he couldn't be here today, but he's in the hospital recovering from a heart episode. He briefed me on the things I should ask you, though, just to make sure. And eventually we'll have a DNA test done so there is no doubt." Keller smiled. "I bet you don't remember me."

Nigel leaned closer. "Kelly?" he asked, and Keller nodded. "We played together when we lived in town before Mom and Dad died." Nigel grinned and turned to Garrett. "Kelly was older than me, but we used to hang out."

Keller chuckled. "His mom and dad used to ask me to babysit them for parties. It was the easiest forty bucks I ever made. We played, ate junk food, hung out—it was a blast. Where's Jules?"

"Playing Candy Crush in the other room. I think he's obsessed," Garrett said as Keller pulled out a stack of papers.

"Your parents' will is very clear. Your uncle was your guardian and trustee until you turned twenty-one. Then you came into your inheritance and have the option of becoming your brother's trustee and guardian. Do you wish to exercise that?"

"If you're asking if I'll take care of Jules, then yes, I will. My uncle can't have anything to do with him. I would have done that when I turned twenty-one if I had known," Nigel stated.

Keller made a few notes. "I know all this sounds really formal, but we have to handle the legalities." She made additional notes. "I need to inform you that the penthouse where you were raised is included. Your uncle is living there now, and we can give him notice to vacate today and…."

Nigel shook his head. "No."

"You want him to live there?" Keller asked.

"Ms. Phipps…," Garrett said.

"Keller, please," she corrected. "And I assume it's okay to call you Garrett." She seemed like a fair enough person.

"Keller, Hilliard has tried to have Nigel and Jules killed on at least three occasions and he kept them on a secluded island for the last eleven years so he could maintain control of their parents' estate. We have plans for Hilliard, so please do not inform him of anything whatsoever. DOJ will handle informing him."

Her mouth hung open and she gasped. "Is that what happened to you?" Suddenly the lawyerly stiffness evaporated. "We had no idea. Your uncle told us that he had sent you and Jules to school in Europe and that you both really liked it there."

"We were taken away and told we were being taken care of by an aunt. Phyllis was good to us, but she was like Fairfield, hired by our uncle. He'll say it was to help protect us, but it was just to keep us on the island so he could control what Mom and Dad left us."

145

"Where are they now?" Keller asked.

"Phyllis is just down the hall. She helped us get away, and Fairfield—" His voice hitched. "—died." Nigel held his chin high, and Garrett was so damned proud of how he handled himself. He took Nigel's hand under the table, sharing his strength.

"Okay. Your uncle has lived in the penthouse for ten years, which would normally allow him to apply for ownership," Keller explained, and Garrett had to calm his impatience. "However, as your trustee he has a fiduciary duty to care for your property and assets… and he can't apply for ownership of assets in his care. So that rule does not apply here." She hummed softly. "He could claim squatter's rights, but that's a stretch considering he is your trustee and shouldn't be benefiting personally from those assets under his trust. There are a lot of arguments to be made, but he's going to have trouble using any of them."

Keller nodded, clearly pleased with her line of reasoning, and passed over sheaves of papers for Nigel to sign. She reviewed each one with him, and Nigel signed his name to them.

"I think we're done."

"Does this mean my uncle doesn't…?" Nigel faltered, his words trailing off in a sigh.

"Hilliard Montague officially has no say or influence in either of your lives any longer. The estate was technically yours when you turned twenty-one. All of this is to make it official and so we can register all the bank accounts, deeds, and properties in your name." Keller gathered the pages. "I'll call you when I get back to the office to inform you when all the papers have been filed." She took out another set of documents. "These prove what we've done today and that all properties are yours now. Once he's in custody, we will take out ads in all financial papers to announce that your uncle no longer speaks for either of you and cannot act in your name in any way. But feel free to handle your uncle in the way you see fit." Keller chuckled. "God, I'd love to be there, but it's best if I stay away. There are rental and tenancy laws that could come into play. It can be tricky, but if I'm not there, then I can't comment on them." She held out her hand, shook Nigel's, and gave him a card. "If there is anything I can do to help, or if you just want to talk, give me a call any time." She smiled. "Maybe you and I can have dinner soon and you can tell me all about this island of yours. I'd love to hear about it." Keller quietly left the room.

Nigel put his head on the table, shoulders shaking. Garrett smoothed his hands over them, being there without talking. "I don't know what I'm going to do," Nigel said quietly. "I don't know anything about companies or apartments, and God knows what else I own now and don't know about."

"I'm sure Keller will help you with all that once you're ready," Garrett said. "Just take things one step at a time." He could say that, but this was overwhelming for him, by proxy.

"I'm trying. But we're alone now." Nigel sat back up, sniffing softly. "Two weeks ago I was happy, collecting my shells on the bottom of the lagoon, checking that they were okay and growing. Now I'm here, the people I thought loved me were paid to be there, my uncle has tried to kill me more than once...." He turned away. "And I met you." Nigel sniffed again. "But you're going to leave, and then what am I going to do?"

Garrett wanted to deny that conclusion, but he couldn't. "I have a job in Baltimore," he said feebly. "It isn't that far away, and there are regular trains. I can come here to visit you, and...." It sounded lame even to him. In the back of his mind, he could hear David scolding him. "Screw that. What do you want me to do? If you want me to stay here with you and Jules, I'll do that. If you want me to go, I'll do that too." The thought of walking away from Nigel made his heart ache almost as much as when he'd first lost David. He had no fucking idea how that could be after just a few weeks, but it was true, and denying it would be stupid as hell.

"I don't know." Nigel swallowed, his eyes filling with doubt and worry. "I want you to stay, but that isn't fair to you. I'm a man now, and I should be able to do what a man does. And I shouldn't ask you to give up your life just because it's what I want." He blinked. "You'll come to hate me for that."

Jules came out of the bedroom and hurried over to show Garrett his game. He was already on level forty-nine. "This is really fun." He plopped down in one of the chairs and went at the game with full concentration, completing the next puzzle in a matter of seconds.

"Why don't you and I talk about this later?" Garrett yawned, and Nigel did the same. "Jules, would you go down the hall and see if Phyllis would like to join us for dinner?" He thought that maybe it was time for him to place an order and try to get settled for the night. It was already nearing eight o'clock.

Jules hurried out the door.

Garrett picked up one of the in-house menus and handed it to Nigel. "Pick whatever you want," he told him.

Phyllis and Jules returned with Jenkins, and Garrett placed the order and Jenkins said he'd deliver it when it arrived. No James Bond–type of switch with the delivery.

"I spent the afternoon being questioned," Phyllis told him once Nigel and Jules were settled for a while.

"Just tell them the truth. You telling them everything only helps them in the fight with Hilliard."

"I know. It was hard, that's all." She sat down, looking more drawn than he had ever seen her.

Once the food arrived, Jenkins brought it in and placed it at the table. They asked if he wanted to stay, but he thanked Nigel and left again.

Dinner itself was quiet, with tired faces and half-lidded eyes meeting others. Even Jules seemed to have run down and was half asleep.

"You should plug in your iPad so it can recharge the battery." Garrett took a break and showed him how to do that. He never thought about such things, but everything was new for them.

"I'm going to go to my room," Jules said, taking his iPad and the cord, giving Phyllis a hug and then leaving the room, closing the door.

"He's going to play that game for hours," Nigel explained.

"It's okay if it makes him happy." Garrett could only imagine how he was feeling right now. "We can check on him later."

Nigel nodded, and Phyllis stood, saying good night. She left the room, and Garrett set the dishes outside in the hallway and bolted the door. Then he turned out the lights, and he and Nigel went into the bedroom. Garrett closed the door and motioned for Nigel to use the bathroom first. Then he took his turn and climbed into bed in his underwear next to him.

It was time for that talk.

CHAPTER 11

GARRETT WAITED for Nigel to step away from the windows. He'd gotten out of bed and started pacing as they talked. Now Nigel was still, just looking. His boxers hung on his hips, and he was the definition of hot. Garrett wasn't going to rush him, and looking kept him plenty happy.

"I can't ask you to stay with us," Nigel said softly. "Though I want to." He turned, and Garrett looked into deep, troubled eyes, as dark as though they'd seen hell. "If I could, I'd ask you to stay here with us and help us figure out what we're going to do and how Jules and I are going to fit into this world." He turned away again, staring out at the lights of the city while Garrett turned off the bedside lamp. "It's prettier than I imagined it would be... and uglier too, I guess."

"What are you going to do?" Garrett asked, his mouth dry.

Nigel shook his head. "I don't know. Jules is young... well, younger, and he deserves a chance to see the world and be a kid. I can't deny him that chance no matter how badly I want to run away." This time when Nigel turned back to him, he looked older, little wrinkles around his eyes.

"Nigel...." Garrett sighed. "My life in Baltimore is pretty shitty, if you want to know the truth. David and I had friends, but after he died, I let most of them go. I couldn't face all of them. It felt wrong and... just wrong." He hung his head. "You know I've been working myself to the bone just to try to forget, and it didn't work." He patted the edge of the bed, and Nigel joined him. "I don't have a life there—I have a job. Big deal. I don't even think I like it that much." Right now, the thought of going back to his empty house and a job that pushed him to the edge of his sanity sounded about as interesting as bashing his finger with a hammer.

"So, you want to stay and help me with this mess." Nigel chuckled.

Garrett leaned forward to wrap his arms around Nigel, tugging him close. "Why don't we take care of your uncle, and then I have to get my stuff from the boat in St. Thomas. We can take things one step at a time." He clutched Nigel to him, their heat melding together. "The thought of going back to work...." He stepped away. "When I first left on this trip, I was so wounded. You...."

"I gave you something to do," Nigel supplied. "I know I'm completely clueless and—"

"That's not what I meant," Garrett interrupted. "You gave me a purpose and woke me out of the blackness that had become my life. I didn't even know how bad things had gotten until I met you." He sighed. "You saved me, you have to know that. I was existing for a long time, but not really living, and you changed that." He tilted Nigel's head upward with the lightest touch on his chin. "You walked onto that beach, and I didn't know what hit me."

"But I didn't do anything," Nigel whined in exasperation.

"Yes, you did. Do you have any idea how you swept me off my feet? You showed me your conch collection and took me camping in the cave. You were generous and kind. I used to sit on that boat, watching for you half the day, just for the chance to see you. I can't remember the last time I looked forward to anything, let alone wanted to get up in the morning. And I did, early... every day... just in the hope that you would walk out of that greenery and make the sun shine again." He shook his head, meeting Nigel's intense gaze. "So don't tell me you didn't do anything."

Nigel smiled and leaned closer. "What do we do from here, then?" He looked around. "I have an apartment here, apparently, but I don't know if this is the right place for us."

"Nigel, you have enough money that you can live anywhere you want. But I suppose there are a number of things you should get straightened out. So why don't we do this? You stay here and figure things out. I'll do what I can to help... and then in the fall, when it starts getting cold, we can fly down to the islands, get a boat, and you can go back."

Nigel actually smiled. "I can?"

"Why not? We can check with Keller to find out who actually owns the island. But if it's your uncle, we can figure out where the money came from, and if it was actually the estate, then we can petition to have it transferred."

Nigel's eyes glassed over.

"In short… yes, you can go home if that's what you want." He smiled, and when Nigel pressed Garrett back on the bed, Garrett laughed as Nigel squirmed on top of him. "You like that idea."

"Yes. I want to see if my shells are okay, and Jules can check for turtles, and we can play in the water." Nigel's eyes darkened even further. "You and I can go back to the cave and camp there again."

The temperature in the room rose by ten degrees. "Is that what you'd like?"

"Yes. Though this time maybe we could figure out how to bring a bed or something." Nigel rolled off and splayed himself on the mattress. "I really like this one. They're so soft. Lots better than sleeping on the sand." He shimmied on the duvet, and Garrett smiled. He loved seeing Nigel happy, and if he could make that happen every day, he could live a happy life.

"You're such a goof, you know that?" Garrett grabbed Nigel, stilling him, slid his arms around his waist, and tugged him close once again. "But you're my goof, and I never want you to change. Not for a second." Nigel was gentle, and Garrett hoped he stayed that way.

Garrett brought their lips together in a kiss that made him forget everything except the man in his arms. Nigel clung to him, and Garrett relished the closeness. After days in the cramped cabin of the boat, with little privacy, he was here in a room of their own with Nigel, a huge, king-size, luxurious bed… and he was so damned tired, he could barely keep his eyes open. Garrett didn't want to back away or bring this to an end, but when they broke their kiss, Nigel rested his head on Garrett's shoulder, lying quietly.

"I'm nervous about tomorrow." He met Garrett's gaze. "And you're going to think me stupid and stuff, but I just want to lie here. You aren't mad, are you?" He blinked, and Garrett rolled them over until Nigel rested on the bed once again. Without asking, he positioned Nigel's head on the pillow and pulled back the covers so he could get in.

"You're not stupid. Sometimes it isn't the time for sex." Opening one's soul and being free to admit one's needs generated a level of trust that could be hard to match, even at the height of passion. "Get into bed, and I'm going to pull the curtains closed. It will block out the light." He slipped off the bed and walked to the window to do so. The fabric dulled the residual sounds of the city and left them in a cocoon of their own.

Garrett climbed back into bed, and just like the other times they were together, Nigel pressed right next to him, arms slipping around his waist.

"Good night," Nigel said, closing his eyes.

Garrett wished him a good night as well. He was bone-tired, and yet he ended up staying awake for what seemed like hours, finally smiling and relaxing, letting go of the tension and loss he'd been holding on to for so damned long.

"I think I can be happy, David," he whispered into the darkness and closed his eyes.

"GARRETT, NIGEL, I'm really hungry," Jules said from the edge of Garrett's consciousness.

Garrett wiped the sleep out of his eyes. "You can order room service. If you bring me the menu we used last night, I can show you how to order." He lay back down, and two seconds later, Jules was back. Garrett showed him the breakfast section, and Jules looked at it with a shrug. "We can get some of everything so you can try it if you want."

"Cool. I'll order." Jules raced away, and Garrett wondered what they were going to get. He pushed back the covers, pulled on one of the white hotel robes, and joined Jules in the living room. "Waffles and pancakes, four glasses of orange juice, coffee, and three bagels." Jules grinned and listened, then hung up the phone. "They said half an hour."

"Okay. I'm going to go get dressed, and after breakfast, I have to buy some fresh clothes."

"Is Nigel up?" Jules asked.

"I think so. Give me a minute and come on in." Garrett returned to the bedroom, grabbed the clothes he had, and went into the bathroom, catching a glimpse as Jules bounded onto the bed.

"I love that we can call on that phone thing and food arrives. It's awesome."

Garrett closed the door and then got into the shower. He was lathering up when the door opened, causing him to jump. He poked his head from behind the curtain as Nigel slipped off his boxers, grinning before sliding past the frosted sliding doors behind him.

"Where's Jules?" Garrett was half afraid he'd bound in here as well.

"In his room, playing that game, waiting for the food like he's starving." Nigel slipped his arms around Garrett's waist, hands blazing a trail of heat that left Garrett breathless and his knees shaking. When he pressed to Garrett, cock sliding along his butt cleft, he reached for the soap dish to steady his balance. "Speaking of starving...." Nigel's voice lowered an octave, growing rumbly and rich.

"What did you have in mind?" Garrett managed to get the soap back in the dish, then turned around, pulled Nigel under the water, and kissed him. Nigel's hair plastered to his head, wetness cascading over them from the rain-shower head. He kept his eyes shut as his cock throbbed between them. Garrett cupped Nigel's butt, bringing them closer together even as Nigel slid downward. "Sweetheart, I...."

Nigel licked and kissed down his belly, and Garrett swallowed hard. Then Nigel closed his lips around the head of Garrett's cock, and his knees shook. He wound his fingers into Nigel's wet hair and cupped his head, then his strong shoulders as Nigel took him deeper.

He tried like hell to stop the whine that burst from him, his heart warming by the second.

Nigel pulled away and slowly stood. Garrett tugged him nearer once again, their warmth mingling under the hot water. Garrett needed him the way he needed air, and Nigel…. God, the thought of letting him go turned Garrett cold for a second. How in the hell could he possibly, ever, not have this… him… love in his life once more? He brought their lips together again, kissing Nigel with everything he had.

"I want you," Nigel whispered against his lips. "I need you."

"I want the same, but I want you in the bed where I can make love to you properly." Garrett cupped the most perfect butt on earth. It was made for his hands. Hell, everything about Nigel seemed made for him.

Nigel stiffened and slowly raised his gaze. "You love me?"

Garrett smiled with a little relief. He'd wondered if something was wrong at first. "Yes, I do." The words came out with an ease that surprised him. He had expected that saying he loved someone other than David would be hard, but with Nigel, it was as easy as pie. "I didn't mean to, but I did. I fell in love with you." He turned off the water and grabbed the towels.

"Are we done?" Nigel squeaked, standing in the middle of the shower, cock pointing upward, his hands on his hips. "What is this? In books, they tell each other that they love each other and then come the really good parts. I feel sort of cheated."

Garrett stepped closer. "Your brother is out there about to bring in breakfast. You know as soon as it arrives, he's going to rush in here, and the last thing I want him to see is you and me…." Garrett swallowed. "Besides…." He slid his fingers around Nigel's cock and stroked slowly. Nigel quivered. "Anticipation is good for the soul." He laughed, and Nigel growled.

But Garrett had no intention of leaving Nigel hanging. He lifted Nigel into his arms, set him on the counter, spread his legs, and swallowed his cock to the root. Nigel shook and moaned softly, cock throbbing as it slid over Garrett's tongue, his rich, earthy flavor bursting in his mouth.

Nigel whined, and Garrett knew things were coming to a conclusion quickly, for him as well. "Garrett...," Nigel whimpered under his breath as he thrust forward, clinging to the edge of the counter. Garrett was already lost in the moment and pushed Nigel and himself to the point of no return, taking him deep as Nigel plunged over the edge, with Garrett right along with him.

Garrett stilled, his pulse racing, head on cloud nine. Nigel breathed like he'd run a marathon. Garrett let Nigel slip from between his lips. Handing him his towel, he used his own to clean himself up.

"Breakfast is here...," Jules called in a singsong way.

Garrett could barely move, but leaned in to kiss Nigel gently. "I do love you."

Nigel sniffed. "I love you too." He turned away. "Just don't ever leave."

Garrett's thoughts came to a screeching halt. "Why would I?"

"What if I'm not good enough?" Nigel asked, with such earnestness that it cut through the postpassion haze like a knife through butter. "Mom and Dad are gone, Aunt Phyllis isn't.... Fairfield tried to kill us.... What if I'm not worth loving?"

"None of that has anything to do with you. Hilliard is an ass, but that isn't your fault, and your mom and dad dying... it was an accident...." As he said the words, a chill raced up his back. Garrett tried to will it away, but it grew colder and harsher by the second. "And none of that says anything about the person you are. And it certainly doesn't mean that I'm going to go running for the hills. Being with you makes me happy—you make me happy."

"Guys, I'm gonna eat it all," Jules teased from the other room, and they finished dressing before joining Jules. He had a huge plate of food in front of him and was downing it fast enough to make any teenager proud.

Garrett poured himself a cup of coffee, and once Nigel had sat down to eat, he snagged a few pieces of fruit before exiting the suite. "Is Carver up?" Garrett asked the agents outside the door.

"He's still resting."

"I need to talk to him, alone." Garrett knocked on the door and was let inside. Carver, still in a robe, his arm pressed to his chest in a sling, joined him. "I didn't want to ask in front of Jules and Nigel, but have you looked into the circumstances of their parents' death? Nigel said it was an accident."

Jenkins, who was dressed and already at his computer, said, "I looked at the file briefly. Their deaths were indeed ruled an accident. They were hit here in the city, broadsided by a huge SUV on Fifth coming through a light. It says their car was a convertible—it ended up crushed under the other vehicle."

"What about the driver? Was he drunk?" Garrett asked.

"No." Jenkins looked up from the screen. "Why?"

Garrett released his breath. "I wonder if Hilliard could have had them killed. He sure as hell seemed to have a plan in place once they were gone. After Jules and Nigel went to the funeral, an 'aunt' met them and escorted them to the island, where they lived for the decade. All he had to know was the route they were taking and have them rammed. What time of day was it?"

"Late. They were coming home from a charity fundraiser," Jenkins supplied. "There is an article in the file from the next day about the event."

"Easy enough to arrange. It was dark, there weren't a huge number of people on the street. Hilliard was probably there—he knew what they were driving. Just a call, and greedy but so far less successful Hilliard gets access to his brother's money." Garrett turned to Carver.

"That's diabolically brilliant and worthy of a movie plot."

"Yes," Jenkins interjected. "The driver had no alcohol in his system. The Montagues had a little, but were well under the limit. The incident was deemed an accident, and that was it." Jenkins continued typing.

"And Hilliard has everything he always wanted," Garrett added sarcastically.

"True. But I don't think we're going to be able to prove anything at this point," Carver said.

Garrett didn't argue with him. He had no basis other than a feeling that wouldn't go away. He sighed. "We're finishing up breakfast and can be ready to go in an hour."

"Excellent," Jenkins said. "We have people watching the building. Hilliard is in the penthouse. His first appointment is at noon today, and he has company… paid company." He smirked. "Make sure the guys are ready, and we'll take you over."

Garrett thanked them and left, the chill in his spine not abating. The situation with Nigel and Jules's parents made him even more nervous. It was a distinct possibility Hilliard had killed his brother and his sister-in-law, and Garrett wondered if he should tell Nigel. The thought of adding more worry and hurt made Garrett's heart ache, and he paused outside the door, nodding to the agent on duty before going inside.

Jules sat on the sofa, the iPad propped up on his knees, playing away. Nigel wasn't about, so Garrett tried to enter the bedroom but found the door locked.

Garrett sat at the end of the sofa, catching Jules's attention. "Do you want to go with us?"

"To skewer my uncle?" Jules grinned and set down the iPad. "You bet. I want to watch him squirm like a bait fish." He actually rubbed his hands together.

Nigel came out of the room and joined them.

"Here's what's happening. I'm going to run down to the lobby to the shop there so I can get some fresh clothes. I won't be long. Then I'm going to dress, and we're going to confront your uncle."

"Can't the lawyer do that?" Nigel asked.

"Man," Jules groaned. "I want to see the old bastard squirm after what he did to us." He sat up, and Garrett suppressed a grin as Nigel's lips drew into a straight line.

"You could have the lawyers do it, but the fastest way is for you to press your claim directly. I'm going to be with you, and so are agents Carver and Jenkins, as well as others. I need both of you to be dressed and ready when I get back, and don't answer the phone or open the door to anyone other than me or the agents. Bolt it on the inside. Okay?" He ruffled Jules's hair, got up, and hugged Nigel before kissing him.

"Do you really have to do that where I can see it?" Jules groused. He was most definitely going to be a handful and was becoming a more typical teenager by the hour. "I'm happy for both of you, though."

Garrett reluctantly released Nigel and hurried for the door.

EVEN THOUGH the penthouse was only a block away from the hotel, they'd taken a car in the interest of safety. Then they lingered in its plush seats, going over the plan one last time.

Phyllis had asked to come as well. The agents had balked, but Jules wanted her along.

They entered the building with Carver and Jenkins following behind.

"May I help you?" the doorman asked from behind the art deco masterpiece of a reception desk. The entire lobby was a study in the art form's splendor, with marble mosaics on the floor and continuing to the walls. It was stunning to say the least.

"We need to access the penthouse," Nigel answered the graying doorman, who looked to be in his midfifties or so.

"I'm sorry, but that's private."

Nigel shifted his weight nervously. "Yes, I know. We used to ride up and down in the private elevator when we were children." He smiled and then leaned forward. "Charlie? I remember you. I'm Nigel."

Charlie's face lit like it was Christmas morning. "My goodness, it's good to see you!" He came from around the desk, grinning before shaking Nigel's hand. "It's been quite a while. I hope you did well in school. Your uncle said you were doing well, whenever I asked."

Nigel tensed even more.

"Nigel and Jules would like to go up to see their uncle," Garrett explained.

159

"I'll call and tell him." Charlie picked up the phone.

"No," Jenkins said forcefully.

"I have to. Only the owner can authorize access," Charlie said, without putting down the phone.

"In that case, that's me. I own the penthouse. Not my uncle. In fact, he has been living here illegally for a year and a half. So, Charlie, you are not to alert my uncle, and please call the elevator so we can go up and pay him a visit."

Damn, Nigel was forceful, and it was awesome to see. And a damned turn-on.

"Are you sure?" Charlie asked.

"Yes. You will not get in any trouble. These men here are with the FBI, and they can make sure of that."

Two more agents entered the building, taking control of the lobby. Charlie stood out of the way as the private elevator at the very back of the lobby opened and the six of them got inside. Nigel pressed the button for the penthouse, and the doors closed and they began to rise.

Jules held Phyllis's hand as they went. He stayed silent as anticipation and nervousness filled the elevator car.

They stepped out into a gorgeous small gold-and-white lobby with a door directly across from the elevators and one to the side.

"That's for the maid and other staff," Nigel said as he looked around and then pointed at the door. "I remember that." He bent to a mark in the corner. "That's where you drew on the stone with magic marker. Mom was so mad, and they tried their best to get it out." He smiled at Jules. Then Nigel knocked firmly on the door and waited. When it didn't open, he knocked again, this time half pounding.

Footsteps thumped on the other side and finally the door opened. "What do you think—" A man in his late fifties, undone tie around his neck, glared at them. "How did you get up here? Never mind. Get back in the elevator or there will be hell to pay." Fire burned in his eyes, and he started to shut the door.

"Uncle Hilliard. I'm Nigel, and this is Jules." He pressed right inside, and Garrett followed. "I have claimed my inheritance, and part

160

of it is this penthouse. Since this is my property, I'm here to move in."
He smiled. "Oh, and I brought some friends with me in case you cause
trouble." So far things were going exactly as planned.

"Boys, it's good to see you." There was no warmth in his voice
at all. "I'll gladly leave, if you give me a little time to move out."

"Actually, you've had eighteen months, and since this is my
apartment, these men are going to help you leave. Gentlemen, since
this is my house, you may go wherever you like."

"Excuse me?" Hilliard said, puffing out his chest. "They aren't
going anywhere."

"Yes, they are." Nigel was magnificent, standing up to his uncle
without batting an eyelash. "See, these men are from the FBI, and
since I am the property owner and you have lived here illegally for
the last year and a half while you held Jules and me prisoner on the
island, I'm granting them permission to look anywhere they like and
search at will. Gentlemen." Nigel waved magnanimously, and Carver
and Jenkins stepped inside. "The penthouse is yours. Go wherever
you like."

"I'm calling my lawyer," Hilliard said.

"Good," Garrett told him. "You're going to need one." He
stood next to Nigel as Carver made a phone call. Soon the elevator
disgorged another six agents, and they fanned out into the penthouse.

"Stay out of my private—"

"Nothing is private when you're living somewhere illegally,"
Garrett interrupted. "You held Jules and Nigel away so you could
keep control of their parents' money."

"I did no such thing!" Hilliard countered. "I took care of them
and gave them an upbringing in an environment where they could be
themselves."

Phyllis, who had stayed in the hallway, stepped through the
door. "Do you want to try again, Mr. Montague?" She glared at
Hilliard with such hatred, Garrett could feel it. "I've already told the
police everything you've done and what you paid Fairfield and me
to do. So you can stop the lying. The picture is clear." She smacked

Hilliard across the face with enough force to send him reeling. "You total bastard."

"You're just as guilty," he countered.

"I didn't try to have them killed," she said, kneeing him in the groin and sending Hilliard to his knees. Then she whirled around and went to the outer hall, standing near the door.

"Mr. Hilliard Montague, I am hereby notifying you that all your personal assets have been frozen by the FBI pending investigation into their source. You are welcome to contact them to determine when the funds will be released, but all bank accounts and holdings are now under their control." Carver smiled, and Garrett swore wisps of smoke might have floated out of Hilliard's ears.

"Stay out of there," Hilliard demanded as the agents pushed open the door to what was obviously an office. "Those are my personal things."

"And it's my room," Nigel countered. "They are welcome to go anywhere."

Garrett wanted to laugh, but he held it together and stayed close to Nigel and Jules in case Hilliard tried anything.

"At least let me get some of my things if you're going to kick me out." Without waiting for permission, he strode down the hallway to the room at the very end and slammed the door.

A pair of agents followed him down the hall. Before they made it halfway, the bedroom door burst open again and Hilliard came out, carrying a gun in each hand. The agents reached for their guns, but Hilliard shot point-blank before they could get them out. He continued down the hall, rounding on Nigel.

Garrett tugged him out of the way and stepped back to the entrance hall. He grabbed Jules and got him around the corner. "Call the elevator and get the hell out of here," he told both of them, shoving them toward it. The doors slid open, and Garrett practically pushed both of them into the lobby, then turned away to stop Hilliard from reaching them.

"Take it easy," Carver said as Hilliard held a gun at both him and Garrett. "Put the guns down. It isn't too late."

But Hilliard was cornered, which was when he'd be at his most dangerous.

He stood still and Garrett could tell he was thinking, trying to figure a way out of this. "You put your guns down. I'm in control here." He glanced around, clearly looking for his way out. Thankfully the boys were out of harm's way and couldn't be used by their uncle for leverage. He took a step back, still holding them at gunpoint. Hilliard was cool, and Garrett figured he had something else up his sleeve.

This guy was off his rocker. Garrett wished he had a weapon, but it would do him no good, as demonstrated by Carver slowly placing his gun on the floor.

"Why did you do it?" Garrett asked to get Hilliard talking. "The boys were eleven and three when their parents died in the accident you arranged. There was no need to send them off anywhere." He glanced around, movement near the edge of the hallway door catching his attention. *Dammit—Phyllis.* He should have made sure she was with the boys, but there hadn't been time.

"Little shits. They were all supposed to have been in that car. They were supposed to go on a family trip." Hilliard curled his lip upward. "Then Giles and Marlie got that damned invitation and decided to go to the benefit. Do you have any idea how long it took to arrange for that fucking accident? That night was fucking perfect, and I could have gotten rid of the whole mess of them." He glanced at Carver. "Now have the others lie down on the floor, or so help me, I'll blow both your brains out."

"Guys...," Carver said, and some of the agents lay down, but others stayed where they were.

"Now!" Hilliard's hands shook, and Garrett saw his finger tighten. He dropped to the ground as the gun pointed at him went off.

"No!" Nigel raced toward him and threw himself on top of Garrett.

Two more shots sounded in rapid succession, then a third, and all was silent. Garrett lifted his head, hoping to hell one of those shots hadn't hit Nigel.

"You okay?" he whispered, and Nigel's weight lifted. Garrett turned to see Hilliard lying on the floor, bleeding from his shoulder onto the white marble. An agent had a bead on him and was already calling for emergency care. Phyllis was splayed on the floor, and Nigel knelt by her side.

"Garrett," Nigel said urgently, helplessly cradling Phyllis's head in his arms. "Why did you do that?" he asked her, cradling her head in his arms. "You ran out and saved me."

"I owed you so much. You and Jules deserve a chance at happiness." She coughed, blood sliding down the sides of her mouth. "Promise me that you won't think badly of me."

Nigel rocked slowly back and forth as Phyllis's eyes drifted closed and her chest stilled.

"Nigel," Garrett said softly.

Nigel placed her head on the floor and backed away. Garrett held him off to the side while the others moved around them in the room. Ambulance workers came and took Hilliard away. The coroner took Phyllis, and then there were questions and statements.... Garrett was familiar with the routine, but it was still difficult, especially on Nigel.

"Let's go back to the hotel. The police are going to need some time here, and they can go through everything in the house."

"Yeah." Nigel got shakily to his feet, and they rode down in the elevator and found Jules waiting in the lobby.

"It's over, Jules. Uncle Hilliard is going to jail. He shot Phyllis."

"Is she going to be okay?" Jules asked, and Nigel shook his head. "Oh."

Nigel hugged his brother. "She saved me and Garrett." He swallowed, and they stood together, holding each other. "Phyllis asked us not to think badly of her." Nigel closed his eyes, and Garrett let the two boys comfort each other.

"Do you want to go back to the hotel?" Garrett asked after a bit.

Nigel nodded, and Garrett led them out of the building and down the street. At least now they could walk out in the open, and the fresh air seemed to do both of them good. They were quiet but less shaken by the time they rode up to the room, and Garrett ordered lunch with plenty of comfort food, including cookies, ice cream, and macaroni and cheese.

"What do we do now?" Jules asked.

"They'll take care of everything in the penthouse, and then we'll have it cleaned and you can move in there if you want. I know it might be hard, and if you don't care to, that's fine. You could sell it."

Nigel shook his head. "No. That place is our only link with Mom and Dad, and who knows, there may be things of theirs inside somewhere."

"But...." Jules seemed a little lost. "Aunt Phyllis...." He stopped and blinked, and Garrett wished he could take all this ache and hurt away.

"Why don't we have lunch and then I'll take you to see some of the city?" He figured a walk in Central Park with its trees and open spaces might help them. But the more he thought about it, the more simplistic and stupid that sounded. Nigel and Jules needed the familiar.

His phone rang, and Garrett pulled it out of his pocket, going to the windows to speak more privately. "Hey, captain."

"How did it go?" he asked, and Garrett flicked his gaze to Nigel. Jules sat nervously, his game next to him. "Wreckley...."

Garrett sighed as Nigel stood near the wall. "It was a disaster. Two agents were shot, but they were wearing vests, so other than some bruising, they were okay. Phyllis was shot, and unfortunately the wounds were fatal." Garrett sighed. "She took the bullet for Nigel and me."

"What about the uncle?"

"He's in custody. His assets are frozen, and Nigel will be working with a lawyer to help identify his next steps. Basically, Hilliard isn't going anywhere for a long time. Not after killing Phyllis in cold blood and admitting he had his brother and sister-in-law killed." Garrett tried to relax a little but was completely unsettled.

"That's good. Not that anyone was hurt, but that he's in custody and the boys are safe." The captain sighed. "So what I need to know is when you're coming back to work."

Garrett paused, then held out his hand to Nigel, who hurried over to him. "I don't know," he answered truthfully. "Nigel needs me here, and…." He took a deep breath. "I don't think I like being a police officer anymore." There, he'd said it. "The more I think about it, the more I realize that when I come back, I'm going to end up in the same place I was when I left. And I don't want that. I need to make a change." Garrett braced for the captain to yell or give him shit.

Instead he chuckled. "Sounds like you found something more important than just work." The last thing Garrett had expected was for the captain to understand. "You still have time left on your vacation. Take it, think about what you want, and we'll talk then."

Garrett thanked him, hung up the phone, and slid it back into his pocket. He rejoined the boys, sitting on the sofa, and explained that he'd just given his notice to his captain.

"You're going to stay?" Nigel asked.

"Yes. I don't want to go back to the life I had." Garrett took a deep breath to quell the nerves that threatened to rise. "It wasn't a real life." He put an arm around Nigel and tugged him closer. "But I am going to need to get a job."

"Why?" Nigel asked with a shrug.

"Because I'm not going to live off your money. I can support myself and my family. And I will." Garrett wasn't a freeloader. He wanted to do something productive. "But all that can be figured out later."

"You always say that," Nigel said. "Why not figure it out now?"

Garrett chuckled. Nigel knew how to make him happy. "Because I need to think about it." He turned away from the window and sat on the love seat against the side wall. "I used to think that being a police officer was who I was. David always told me that I was more than that, but I didn't listen. Now I think he was right." At the very least, being a cop didn't hold the appeal it once did, and now that the pressure was gone, he knew he didn't want it back.

166

"You could become a private detective like Sam Spade," Nigel offered. "Wear those cool hats and a trench coat, looking for the Maltese Falcon or maybe treasure." Nigel grinned and sat down next to him. "Or you could stay here and just be with me." He put his arms around Garrett's waist and leaned on his shoulder.

"I couldn't do only that." Hell, Garrett had choices now that he could have only dreamed of. The ability to do whatever he wanted. That could be a dream come true in itself. "But I'll figure it out."

Sometimes things had a way of making themselves clear.

THEY SPENT much of the day talking. Garrett listened a lot and let the guys vent and work through the journey they had been on. He thought at some point they might want professional help, but they weren't ready for that. Nigel and Jules had to be given the chance to grieve for the life they'd thought they had, for Phyllis, and even in a way, for their parents. Garrett determined that he would tell them about their uncle and their parents, but not at the moment. They had enough on their plates right now... but he'd do it soon.

"Do you want to sleep in here alone?" Garrett asked Nigel once Jules had gone to bed. It was late, and they had stayed up watching *Singin' in the Rain*. They all needed some happy, and nothing said happy like Debbie Reynolds.

Nigel shook his head and pulled his shirt up and off. "I want to feel alive, like I did back home." He pushed off his pants and stepped out of the pile of clothing, leaving it on the floor and him naked. "If I could have anything, it would be to feel the way I did on the island, just the two of us, without a care or worry." Nigel closed the distance between them. "Can we do that?"

"Yes." Garrett stripped just as quickly and took Nigel in his arms. "I remember the first time I held you." Things had been so much simpler, and it felt like a lot more than just a few weeks ago. "I think I always will."

"I know I will." Nigel guided him back until Garrett reached the edge of the bed. He'd go anywhere Nigel wanted, and right now they had the same idea. Nigel wrapped his arms around Garrett's waist, and Garrett pulled him close. Having Nigel pressed to him, holding tightly, thrusting his hips so Nigel's cock slid along his belly, was heady in the extreme. Garrett adored the scent of him, the taste and touch of his smooth skin on his hands. He closed his eyes, memorizing every part of Nigel… just in case. He'd been through way too much to take anything for granted.

"I have things for us." Garrett moaned softly as Nigel shimmied his hips.

"What sort of things?" Nigel asked, and Garrett lost the ability to think. Nigel giggled and pushed him backward, sending them both tumbling onto the bed. It felt good to laugh, to let off the weight that had settled on them, almost without realizing it was there until it was gone. Regardless of what had happened, Hilliard was gone, there were no more threats, and Nigel could live his life in the open, the way he wanted. And to think that he wanted Garrett. What could possibly be better than that?

"Things we need so I can make love to you," Garrett whispered, and rolled Nigel onto his back. He took those swollen lips in a powerful kiss before getting up and hurrying to the bathroom. He found the bag of things he'd gotten when he bought fresh clothes and returned, setting them on the nightstand. "Do you know…? Are you sure?"

"I know what men do. I saw it." Color rose in his cheeks, and Nigel pointed to the iPad. "I found some videos, and they showed everything."

Garrett gaped, speechless. "You've had the internet for a little over a day and you already found porn?"

"I wanted to know what two men did together, and this site was really helpful. They were really short, because I didn't have a credit card, but it was enough." Nigel laughed nervously and turned eight shades of red all at once.

Garrett prowled toward the bed. "Did you like what you saw?"

Nigel nodded, his gaze locked on Garrett's. "They were pretty men, but none of them as handsome as you." The sweet talker. "And they screamed a lot. At first I thought they were hurting... but then I knew it was because they were hot to trot."

Where that expression came from, Garrett had no idea, and he had to stop the laughter that threatened to bubble up. He didn't want to spoil the mood, and when Nigel wound his arms around his neck, tugging him downward, Garrett forgot everything else.

Nigel circled his legs around Garrett's waist, and Garrett stroked his palms over Nigel's butt. Garrett teased him open as they kissed, swallowing each other's moans, feeding them back as the heat and passion rose by the second.

Little whimpers filled the air as Garrett stroked Nigel's hot skin, wanting to go slow, but everything inside him said to make Nigel his and pushed him forward. They might be in a fancy hotel, with soft sheets and a perfect bed, but part of him was back on that beach, in the cave, making love to Nigel for the first time. He just had to have him.

Garrett fumbled in the darkness until he found the bag, got to the small tube of slick, and worked it onto his fingers and then into Nigel, his heat and pressure around him for the first time. He knew magic wasn't real. Garrett couldn't snap his fingers and make anything he wanted happen. Except he was wrong—magic was real, and he was holding the source of it, feeling its heat, listening as Nigel moaned and whispered the words that opened his heart. All that existed was Nigel.

"God, I love you," Garrett said without hesitation.

"I love you too." Nigel held him tighter as Garrett slid a finger deeper inside him, splaying his hands against his cheeks, caressing and touching, opening, preparing, making Nigel ready for him.

"Nigel... I...." Garrett's throat dried out as he tumbled into the sea blue of Nigel's eyes.

"I'm ready," Nigel whispered.

Garrett nodded, found a condom, slipped it on, and gently, carefully, against every instinct that pressed him forward, pushed into Nigel. "That's it," Nigel encouraged, and Garrett lost the ability to talk or think about anything other than the night in the cave, lost in Nigel's eyes just as he was now, losing himself in him and never wanting to be found.

"Don't stop," Nigel begged, and Garrett couldn't have if he tried.

He moved slowly, sighing with each slippery slide, taking in each gasp, moan, and breath that Nigel took. They were more explanatory, more precious than any words, because they came from Nigel's core. Each hitch said *yes*, a groan... *more*, a moan... *still more*... and the cries, those he would hear in his sleep, in his dreams for the rest of his life.

"Garrett... I...." Nigel gasped and held still, clutching him as he closed his eyes, pleasure, bliss, and ecstasy written all over his face as he came.

Garrett watched in rapt wonder, holding himself at bay for just a minute longer so he could watch the flush and the surprise of openmouthed pleasure, knowing it was for him. Then, when Nigel opened his eyes, Garrett lost himself in them again, plummeting into his own wave of sweet release, letting Nigel see just how much he undid him.

CHAPTER 12

"ARE YOU sure you're ready to do this?" Garrett asked as the three of them stood near the hotel room door three days later. Together they had seen many of the popular sights in the city and gone to the park each afternoon so Jules and Nigel could be outside. They'd explored every path and corner as though on a treasure hunt.

Garrett had gotten in touch with the owner of the sailboat he'd rented and explained some of the situation. Agent Carver had already arranged for the removal of the guns and to have Garrett's things sent to him. So everything was all fixed on that end at least.

The police had finished with the apartment, and Charlie had helped Nigel get cleaners in there so the place would hold no residue of what had happened, other than memories.

"Yes. I have to." Nigel stood tall at the door. "I won't let Hilliard take anything more away from us. That penthouse was our parents' home, and Jules and I are going to go over there. I don't want to live in this room anymore." He pulled open the door, marched down the hall, and called the elevator. Garrett and Jules followed behind.

"I don't have any memories of the apartment," Jules said. "It's like Nigel expects me to."

"I don't think so. But maybe when you're there, you'll figure out that you do remember something. Maybe even something about your Mom and Dad. It's possible."

Jules didn't seem convinced and loped down the hall. "I really want to go home. Maybe there will be more turtles and I can explore the beach."

The elevator doors opened, and they stepped inside.

"I understand." Garrett turned to Nigel. "What do you think about going back to the island in a few months? It will be colder here, and I bet we'll all be ready for warmer weather." He'd gotten jackets and sweatshirts for them all when the first fall cold front had blown through, knocking the warmer weather away, at least temporarily. "You can have some things with the estate set, and you should be able to be away for a period of time."

Jules practically bounced off the walls of the elevator car, and Nigel nodded, looking at him as though he hung the moon.

"How long before you have to go back to Baltimore?" Nigel asked as they reached the bottom and the doors slid open.

"You aren't staying?" Jules asked, deflating like a balloon.

"I have things I have to tie up there, but I'm not going to leave until both of you are settled with a place to live. I promise. Then I'll be back." Garrett took Nigel's hand and kept it as they walked to the penthouse building, where Charlie called the elevator.

The ride upward was tense, growing more so the longer they were in the elevator.

"You don't have to stay if you don't want to," Garrett reminded them.

The car came to a stop and the doors opened to the small entrance lobby. They stepped out, and Nigel unlocked the apartment door.

It looked much the same but smelled of disinfectant. There were no signs of what had happened. The floors gleamed. Garrett closed the door while the guys stood looking around.

"I remember this," Nigel said softly. "I used to play right here on the floor with my cars and trucks. Dad hated it, but the floors were so smooth that they could really go." He took a few steps farther into the space. "But none of this furniture was my parents'. Except that." He pointed to a corner. "I remember being afraid of the bear."

Garrett smiled at the large openmouthed bronze bear. He could see it scaring a kid. "So that belonged to your parents'?"

Nigel nodded, pointing again. "That did too, and so did the side table over there. I remember those. But the rest must be Uncle Hilliard's."

"Anything you don't want can be removed. And you can go shopping or hire a decorator for anything else you want."

Nigel shrugged. "I don't really care. Just get his stuff out of here." The large, supple leather sofas looked comfortable enough, and the other furniture was modern and relatively bland. Garrett was pretty sure it was expensive, but it lacked any sort of style.

Jules wandered off down the hall, and Garrett peeked into the office. The desk drawers were closed, but when Garrett looked inside, he found them largely empty. The richly paneled room, with book-matched wood insets, was stunning. "Do you remember this room?" Garrett asked, and Nigel stepped in and gasped softly.

"Dad used to sit behind that desk, and he'd work at night. I used to hide under there, and sometimes Dad would put me on his lap and read me stories." He turned around, the light in his eyes fading a little. "There were always books for me on those shelves. Dad used to read to me all the time. It was one of the things we did together."

Jules came in.

"Do you remember being in here? You sat on Mom's lap and I sat on Dad's, and he read us stories sometimes."

"*Peter Rabbit*," Jules said, and Nigel nodded.

"That was your favorite. You used to put your hand over your face whenever Mr. McGregor entered the story." They shared a smile. "See, you do remember."

"I guess." Jules's lips cocked upward.

"Let's see the rest," Nigel said, and they continued through the apartment. The first two bedrooms were rather neutral, probably for guests. The master had been thoroughly rummaged through by the investigators. "What do we do with all this?"

"We can give it all to charity. I'll call someone, and they can pick it up." Garrett was determined to wipe as much of Hilliard out of the place as possible. "Then you can shop for the kind of bed you want."

"That *we* want," Nigel corrected, threading his arm through Garrett's. "Pick any room you want, Jules."

A knock on the front door startled them. Garrett shared a glance with Nigel before going to see who it was.

"Agent Carver," Garrett said brightly as he let him inside. "How's the arm?"

"Better. Thanks." Carver closed the door. "I was stopping by to check on the cleanup job, and Charlie told me you were here already."

Nigel joined them, once again threading his arm with Garrett's.

"We're trying to figure out what to do with Hilliard's things," Garrett explained.

"Somehow I don't really think it's going to matter. He never married and had no children, and he isn't going to be going anywhere for a very long time. We found plenty of evidence in his files, and the list of charges is growing by the hour. I suggest you have them packed up, put them in storage, and send him the information and a bill for the expenses. After that, it's up to him."

Nigel nodded. "I think we can do that."

Carver made a call and set it up. He smiled and hung up. "Someone will be here tomorrow to take care of it. Just tell them what you want to go, and it will be taken care of. I'll make sure Hilliard gets the information." He seemed more than happy. "My advice is to clear out everything that was his and make this place your own. This is a one-of-a-kind place here in New York."

"In more ways than one," Garrett added. "Thank you for all your help."

"What are your plans going forward? Have you thought about it?" Carver looked square at Garrett. "Because we could use a good man like you at the bureau."

Garrett's stomach tightened. Once, an offer like that would have been his dream, but now…. "Thank you, but I think I'm going to try to find something closer to home." He turned to Nigel. "Our home." That was all that mattered. Garrett drew Nigel a little nearer.

Carver smiled and nodded knowingly. "I don't blame you at all." He looked around the area. "It looks like they did a good job."

"They did," Nigel said. "Thank you for everything you did for us."

Carver smiled. "No. Thank you. Your courage to stand up to him and let us inside made all the difference in the world. We've known his business dealings haven't been squeaky clean for some time, but to have the proof…. Your uncle was the kind of man who gives everyone in his profession a bad name." He handed Garrett and Nigel each a business card. "Don't hesitate to call if you run into anything else."

Jules raced in and skidded to a stop as he approached. "I was going to go to the bathroom and I opened the door I thought was it, but it's another room." He grabbed Nigel's arm and tugged him back.

"Thank you for everything." Garrett shook the agent's hand.

"No problem. I have to go." Carver smiled and left the apartment.

Garrett closed the door behind him before following the dual sneezes down the hall.

The room was covered in dust, which had been disturbed only recently, probably by the agents. Garrett opened two of the windows for some fresh air, and the wind rushed through, kicking up more dust. He closed the door and let the wind do its job, carrying much of the dust from the small room, probably a nursery when the apartment was built. It didn't take long for the air to clear.

"What is this?" Jules asked.

Nigel was already digging through boxes. Six had been opened and pushed to the side. With the next, he pulled out some old framed pictures. He held them up, practically jumping up and down, before showing them to Jules. "This is all of us. Mom, Dad, me, and you as a baby." He handed it to Jules and pulled out three more. The rest of the box was paper and packing. Nigel turned into a whirlwind, going through each of the boxes, as well as the closet. Everything else seemed to belong to Hilliard, but in that one box, Nigel and Jules had struck gold.

Garrett pulled Nigel into a hug, and Nigel clung to him, burying his face in Garrett's shirt, crying, grieving. The sobs were wrenching, and Garrett could only imagine the loss upon loss that was coming out all at once. "It's okay. You let it all out." He turned to Jules, who stood all alone, trying to hold himself together. Garrett opened an arm, and Jules joined Nigel, the two of them hugging each other and Garrett. In a way, he was very relieved. It was time they both let out everything they'd been holding inside.

Jules was the first to back away, rubbing his eyes and then leaving the room.

"I found what's left of my parents," Nigel said after a few minutes more. "It isn't much, but it's something." He turned, looking down at the framed pictures: three smiling faces glowing out of the frame, Jules asleep in his mother's arms. "I read somewhere that we get two families. The one we're born with, and the one we make for ourselves."

Garrett nodded, not trusting his voice at the moment. "That's true," he finally managed to say.

"I don't have the family I was born with. Other than Jules, they're gone." Nigel pulled in a deep breath. "Will you be part of the family we make for ourselves?" Nigel nearly broke down again as he said the words.

Garrett pulled him into another hug. "I think I already am."

EPILOGUE

NIGEL STOOD on the deck of the speed boat, practically jumping out of his skin as the island, his and Jules's island, came into view. They had hired a boat and crew from Martinique to bring them over. Aerial pictures of the island showed that the boat Fairfield had used to come and go was still there, so they should have transportation off the island again once they decided to leave.

"I'm ready to be home," Jules said. His energy had built up once the snow began to fly. The first day he had been so excited to check it out, but after he'd felt how cold it was, the winter wind in New York had both him and Nigel running indoors and turning up the heat to near tropical. Granted, Garrett loved getting to snuggle next to Nigel at night, keeping him warm and toasty.

"I know. Both of you were." All Garrett had had to see was the two of them staring out of the windows, frowns on their faces as they watched the snow fall from the penthouse, wrapping their arms around themselves as though the cold was going to reach out and take them at any moment.

"How long are we staying?" Jules yelled to Nigel.

"Two months," Nigel answered. "By then it will be early spring back in New York, and I will have things I need to do."

Garrett was so proud of Nigel, he could bust. He had worked for months to get his parents' things in order and untangled from his uncle's. All of Hilliard's dealings had come under such scrutiny, and the lawsuits were still being filed, so his assets were sold to pay restitution. Nigel had stepped into a role at his father's company, mostly to learn the business and to help oversee his own finances. It was a big job, and Nigel had grown into it more and more each and every day.

At the cove near the house, they dropped anchor, and Royston used the dinghy to ferry them, their supplies, and their gear onto land.

"Thank you," Nigel called to Captain Royston.

"You call if you need anything." He waved as he took the dinghy back and secured it behind the boat. The three of them waved in return and then started lugging everything up to the house.

It hadn't changed much, other than the jungle had tried to make its own inroads into the cleared space around it. Garrett added "cleaning up the property" to the list of things he'd do while he was here.

Nigel pulled open the door and stepped inside. Jules and Garrett followed. Everything was pretty much as they's left it, except for the wounded, who no longer lay on the floor, though the slight remnants of the bloodstains were proof enough of what had happened. Garrett had arranged for Maria from the village to look after the place while Nigel was gone, so it was reasonably clean.

"Carry your things upstairs, and I'm going to get things settled in here."

"I'll put away the kitchen stuff and make us lunch after I unpack," Jules volunteered. He had developed cooking aspirations and seemed at home in the kitchen.

"Wonderful. And don't forget that you have lessons on Monday," Nigel added, and Jules groaned, all melodramatic teenager as he lugged his and Nigel's bags upstairs.

Garrett had brought equipment to replace what he'd put out of commission, including a small satellite dish so they could have regular communication and internet service. The tutors they had hired would hold Skype lessons with Jules when they weren't visiting.

Funny how easy it was to get people to visit when you owned an island in paradise.

"What about the things in Aunt Phyllis's room?" Jules called down the stairs. Both he and Nigel kept referring to her as their aunt. Even in Garrett's sometimes jaded mind, she deserved to be remembered that way.

"What do you think?" Garrett called to Nigel as he rummaged in the kitchen for a bucket, cleanser, and a brush. He found both in the adjacent laundry area and filled the bucket from the sink.

"I'd like to give whatever is good to the village. See if there is anyone there who can use it," Nigel answered, coming up behind him. "Then maybe we can turn the room into a sitting room. It has great windows and air flow, so I'd like to make a reading room out of it." Nigel's love of books hadn't diminished, and his iPad was now full of them, as was one of the boxes he'd brought.

"It sounds wonderful. Whatever you'd like will make me happy. Maybe we could do that, and I could use it as an office while I'm here."

"Perfect. I can read while you work." The glint in Nigel's eye told him that whatever he had in mind didn't involve much work getting done.

"I'm unpacked and going to make lunch so I can go out to the beach." Jules pounded down the stairs as he raced toward the kitchen. Garrett figured lunch was going to consist of whatever Jules could get his hands on quickly. Not that he blamed him. Garrett had a particular beach in mind himself.

"Just go. Garrett and I can make our own lunch when we're hungry," Nigel called as he headed upstairs. Jules ran past Garrett as he took another stab at getting the dried blood off the floorboards. A little of it came out, but he knew some would become part of the wood. He made a note to replace them.

The door banged closed, and Jules was probably halfway to the beach by the time Garrett had a chance to caution him. Not that it mattered. Jules was at home here and knew every stone, each spit of sand.

Nigel bustled down the stairs and opened all the windows to let through the ocean breeze. Then he began cleaning up as well, brushing off cushions and wiping down the furniture. Once Garrett had gotten up what he could, he dumped the dirty water and rinsed the bucket out. When he returned, he found Nigel in the downstairs sitting room, staring at the table.

"What is it?" Garrett asked, following Nigel's gaze.

"These." He picked up a shell and rolled it carefully in his hand. "I gave this to Aunt Phyllis." He turned it over, and a delicate shell necklace toppled out into his hand. "I made this too, from pieces of shell that I shaped from the beach, years ago. She kept it." He seemed surprised.

"She loved both of you. I don't doubt that now." From the expression on Nigel's face, he had been, but that was being swept aside before his eyes. Garrett sat down in the chair across from Nigel. "There's something I have to tell you. That I've been dreading telling you for months."

"I know. You tried to get me out of the room, but I heard Uncle Hilliard." Nigel set down the shell pieces and came to him. "I heard him confess to what he did to Mom and Dad."

Garrett was both relieved and pissed that he hadn't had this conversation earlier. "Does Jules know?"

"No. There's no need to tell him. It won't change anything, and he isn't coming back… ever. Why let him hurt us some more?"

Garrett got up and put his arms around Nigel's waist and leaned on his chest, Nigel winding his fingers in his hair.

"I love you, Garrett, for trying to protect us, but I can handle things on my own now."

"I know," Garrett said. "Sometimes I'm afraid of how capable you are. What if you don't need me, and…?" So much of their time together had been Nigel needing him.

"I'll always *want* you, and that's better." Nigel leaned down and kissed him. "How about we leave this stuff here and head down to the beach… our beach… and I can show you just how much I need and want you?"

How could Garrett say no to making love, with his love, in paradise?

ANDREW GREY is the author of nearly 100 works of Contemporary Gay Romantic fiction. After twenty-seven years in corporate America, he has now settled down in Central Pennsylvania with his husband, Dominic, and his laptop. An interesting ménage. Andrew grew up in western Michigan with a father who loved to tell stories and a mother who loved to read them. Since then he has lived throughout the country and traveled throughout the world. He is a recipient of the RWA Centennial Award, has a master's degree from the University of Wisconsin-Milwaukee, and now writes full-time. Andrew's hobbies include collecting antiques, gardening, and leaving his dirty dishes anywhere but in the sink (particularly when writing). He considers himself blessed with an accepting family, fantastic friends, and the world's most supportive and loving partner. Andrew currently lives in beautiful, historic Carlisle, Pennsylvania.

Email: andrewgrey@comcast.net
Website: www.andrewgreybooks.com

ALL FOR YOU

ANDREW GREY

The only path to happiness is freedom: the freedom to live—and love—as the heart wants. Claiming that freedom will take all the courage one young man has… but he won't have to face it alone.

In small, conservative Sierra Pines, California, Reverend Gabriel is the law. His son, Willy, follows his dictates… until he meets a man in Sacramento, and then reunites with him in his hometown—right under his father's nose.

Reggie is Sierra Pines's newly appointed sheriff. His dedication to the job means not flaunting his sexuality, but when he sees Willy again, he can't escape the feeling that they're meant to be together. He'll keep Willy's secret until Willy is ready to let the world see who he really is. But if going up against the church and the townspeople isn't enough, the perils of the work Reggie loves so much might mean the end of their romance before it even gets off the ground….

www.dreamspinnerpress.com

RUNNING
TO YOU

ANDREW GREY

Home, love, and possibilities he never imagined are waiting for Billy Joe to claim them. But first he needs to escape the horrors of his past.

A twisted act of cruelty and prejudice drives Billy Joe from his Mississippi home, and he makes it as far as Pennsylvania—where his car breaks down just as the year's first snowstorm blows in. Fortunately, Carlos is there to lend a hand.

Carlos is no stranger to hardship. His family rejected him for being gay, but with determination, he put himself through school and became a librarian. Carlos sees the same willpower in Billy, and he wants to help Billy and his son succeed in a new life that is very different from the one they left behind. With his support, they start to adjust, and before long, both men want more than encouragement from each other. They want the chance for a future together, but their families have other ideas… and Billy's will stop at nothing to get what they want.

www.dreamspinnerpress.com

FIRE AND FLINT
ANDREW GREY

CARLISLE
DEPUTIES
1

A Carlisle Deputies Novel

Jordan Erichsohn suspects something is rotten about his boss, Judge Crawford. Unfortunately he has nowhere to turn and doubts anyone will believe his claims—least of all the handsome deputy, Pierre Ravelle, who has been assigned to protect the judge after he received threatening letters. The judge has a long reach, and if he finds out Jordan's turned on him, he might impede Jordan adopting his son, Jeremiah.

When Jordan can no longer stay silent, he gathers his courage and tells Pierre what he knows. To his surprise and relief, Pierre believes him, and Jordan finds an ally… and maybe more. Pierre vows to do what it takes to protect Jordan and Jeremiah and see justice done. He's willing to fight for the man he's growing to love and the family he's starting to think of as his own. But Crawford is a powerful and dangerous enemy, and he's not above ripping apart everything Jordan and Pierre are trying to build in order to save himself….

www.dreamspinnerpress.com

POLICE

FIRE AND GRANITE

ANDREW GREY

A Carlisle Deputies Novel

The heat is growing from the inside, but danger is building on the outside.

Judge Andrew Phillips runs a tight ship in his courtroom. He's tough, and when he hands down a sentence, he expects to be obeyed. So when a fugitive named Harper escapes and threatens his life, Andrew isn't keen on twenty-four/seven protection… especially not from Deputy Clay Brown. They have a past, one that could cause problems in their careers.

But with Clay assigned to Andrew and the two of them together every minute, there's nowhere to hide from their attraction—or from the fact that there's much more than chemistry blooming between them. As the threat intensifies, Clay knows he'll do anything it takes to protect the people who are taking their places in his heart: Andrew and his young niece and nephew.

www.dreamspinnerpress.com

Made in United States
Orlando, FL
22 March 2026

79559117R00115